OURSELVES ALONE
with THE LONG MARCH
and A WOMAN CALLING

OURSELVES ALONE
with
THE LONG MARCH
and
A WOMAN CALLING

ANNE DEVLIN

faber and faber
LONDON · BOSTON

First published in 1986
by Faber and Faber Limited
3 Queen Square London WC1N 3AU

Photoset by Wilmaset Birkenhead Merseyside
Printed in Great Britain by
Whitstable Litho Ltd Whitstable Kent

British Library Cataloguing in Publication Data

Devlin, Anne
Ourselves alone; The long march; and, A woman calling.
I. Title II. Devlin Anne
822'914 PR6054.E921

ISBN 0-571-13874-8

CONTENTS

OURSELVES ALONE

For Chris Parr with love

AUTHOR'S NOTE

I began this play with two women's voices – one funny and one serious – and then I found I had a third – the voice of a woman listening. And all the women were in some ways living without men. And then the father and a stranger came into the room. And I found myself wondering who the stranger was and what he was doing there. And I set the play in Andersonstown because once, I used to live there – and I still do.

August 1985

CHARACTERS

FRIEDA	Sister to Josie, under 25 years
JOSIE	Sister to Frieda, under 29 years
DONNA	Friend to both sisters, Liam's common-law wife, under 30
MALACHY	Father to Frieda, Josie and Liam
LIAM	Malachy's son, Donna's common-law husband
GABRIEL	Cousin to Frieda, Josie and Liam
JOE CONRAN	The Englishman
CATHAL O'DONNELL	Josie's lover, a member of the Provisional IRA
JOHN MCDERMOT	A member of the Workers' Party
DANNY MCLOUGHLIN	A musician
FIRST MAN	A helper in the club
SECOND MAN	In the fight outside the club
FIRST POLICEMAN	In the park, and in Donna's house
SECOND POLICEMAN	In the park
FIRST SOLDIER	In Donna's house
SECOND SOLDIER	In Donna's house

Time: Act 1 is set in late summer; Act 2 autumn into winter.
Duration: eight months.
Setting: mainly Andersonstown, West Belfast; but also Dublin, a hotel room, and JOHN MCDERMOT's house in South Belfast, near the university and the Botanic Gardens.

Ourselves Alone was co-produced at the Liverpool Playhouse Studio on 24 October 1985 and at the Royal Court Theatre Upstairs, London, on 20 November 1985.

Cast in order of appearance:

DANNY	Liam de Staic
FRIEDA	Hilary Reynolds
GABRIEL	Mark Lambert
JOSIE	Brid Brennan
DONNA	Lise-Ann McLaughlin
MALACHY	John Hewitt
JOE CONRAN	Peter Chelsom
JOHN McDERMOT	Adrian Dunbar
CATHAL O'DONNELL	Adrian Dunbar
LIAM	Mark Lambert

All other parts played by the Company

Director	Simon Curtis
Designer	Paul Brown

ACT ONE

SCENE I

FRIEDA, DANNY, GABRIEL, FIRST MAN. *The setting is a club, the centre of Republican activity, political and social, in West Belfast. The period of Republicanism in the post-hunger-strike days is set by the wall hangings; the traditional prominence of Pearse and Connolly has given way to the faces in black and white of ten men: Sands, Hughes, McCreesh, O'Hara, McDonnell, Hurson, Lynch, Doherty, McElwee, Devine.*

It is early evening, the lights in the club are down, the surroundings are not so visible. FRIEDA, *a singer, and* DANNY, *a musician, are rehearsing.*

FRIEDA: (*Sings.*)

> Armoured cars and tanks and guns
> came to take away our sons
> every man should stand beside
> the men behind the wire.

(*Throws the paper down.*)
I don't want to sing this any more!
(*Behind them and around them two men are coming in and out with boxes and stacking them in every available space.*)

DANNY: (*Stops playing.*) Why not?
FRIEDA: Because it's about a man.
DANNY: The song's about Internment, Frieda!
FRIEDA: I'm fed up with songs where the women are doormats!
DANNY: It's a Republican classic!
FRIEDA: I want to sing one of my own songs.
DANNY: But your songs are – not as popular as this one.
FRIEDA: You told me the next time we got a job here you'd let me sing one of my own songs! Just one.
DANNY: (*Sighs.*) Which one did you want to sing?
FRIEDA: I've rewritten 'The Volunteer'.
(*She starts getting a paper out of her bag by the piano.*)

DANNY: All right. I'll look at it when we've rehearsed this.
FRIEDA: Oh Danny. I knew you would.
DANNY: OK. Let's go again.
FRIEDA: (*She sings the first verse of 'The Men Behind The Wire'.*)

Armoured cars and tanks and guns
came to take away our sons –

DANNY: (*Stops.*) Frieda! Do you have to sound so pleased about it? Armoured cars and tanks and guns!
FRIEDA: But the tempo's fast and lively.
DANNY: Absolutely. You have to work hard against that tempo. Again! (*She sings. She stops. The men carrying boxes are now piling them nearer* FRIEDA.) Just a minute . . . Are you going to be much longer shifting that stuff around?
GABRIEL: Nearly finished.
FRIEDA: (*Looking into the box* GABRIEL *has put down*) What is it anyway?
GABRIEL: Bandages.
FRIEDA: In all of them?
GABRIEL: (*Nods.*) I think so. (*The* FIRST MAN *comes in with a larger box, his last.*)
FRIEDA: What are you trying to do – start a fight? (*Calls out.*) Hey wee fella, what have you got in your box?
FIRST MAN: (*Reading off the lid*) Cotton wool balls.
FRIEDA: I always thought there was something funny about you.
FIRST MAN: (*On his way out*) See you wee girl, come the revolution, you'll be the first one up against the wall!
FRIEDA: Well, I hope it's in the nicest possible way.
GABRIEL: What were you looking for?
FRIEDA: Sugar.
GABRIEL: Maybe next week.
DANNY: Frieda!
(*She clears her throat, takes up her position. The men depart. She sings the song again completely.*)

SCENE 2

DONNA, JOSIE, FRIEDA, MALACHY, JOE. JOSIE *is sitting in the dark in a room. Footsteps quickly approach the door.* DONNA *comes in and turns on the light.*

DONNA: Josie! What are you doing sitting in the dark? You've let the fire out.
(JOSIE *laughs.*)
What's so funny?
JOSIE: My daddy used to say, well close the door quickly and keep it in.
DONNA: Used to say? (*Takes her coat off and sits down.*) You couldn't wait to get away from him.
JOSIE: I know.
DONNA: Is everything all right? You were sleepwalking again last night.
JOSIE: Was I?
DONNA: It's the third time this week. I opened my eyes and there you were. Standing over the cot, looking at Catherine.
JOSIE: Was I?
DONNA: You gave me an awful fright.
JOSIE: I'm sorry.
DONNA: I wouldn't have said anything, but I'm afraid of you waking Catherine. It takes so long to get her to sleep these days.
JOSIE: I think I was dreaming about my mother.
DONNA: Was she quiet for you?
JOSIE: Who?
DONNA: Catherine. Was she quiet while I was out?
JOSIE: Yes.
DONNA: I'll just take a wee look in.
JOSIE: She's asleep! I wish I could sleep like that.
DONNA: What's wrong?
JOSIE: I feel sick all the time now.
DONNA: Is it him?
JOSIE: I can't live like this any more. I sit here night after night

wondering will he come tonight.

DONNA: We're all waiting on men, Josie.

JOSIE: If he has to go away for any other reason but her I can stand it.

DONNA: Have you told him this?

JOSIE: No. Of course not. I don't want him to think I care.

DONNA: Aye, but it strikes me that if you were the one with a wife, he might care. Has he ever talked about her?

JOSIE: No.

DONNA: Well I expect she waits too, Josie.

JOSIE: Thanks.

DONNA: At least you have his love.

JOSIE: Love? It's such a silly word. We've never spoken it. It's just that when I'm totally me and he's totally him we swop. Do you know what I mean? (*Pause.*) His arrival is the best time. It's his mouth on my neck, his cool fingers touching me – I make it last right up until he has to leave. And then I row, I fight, I do everything I can to keep him with me and when I hurt him I hurt myself. It's as if we're driven, that bed is like a raft and that room is all the world to us.

DONNA: You're lucky you can feel like that, you might not if you had to live with him.

JOSIE: Live with him? I've dreamt of nothing else.

DONNA: He frightens me Josie – he's not like any man I know.

JOSIE: No he's not.

DONNA: The things I've heard about him. He's a spoiled priest.

JOSIE: Sure I wanted to be a nun once.

DONNA: Aye when you were ten years old. But he's actually been trained as a priest. (*Pause.*) They told him when they blew up the police station near the cemetery that morning that some of our people might get hurt as well. And he asked – how many?

JOSIE: You don't know what you're talking about. Our force is defensive!

DONNA: I'm looking at you but it's him who's talking. I wish I didn't know any of this. I wish I hadn't walked into the room that night and seen you both. I wish you hadn't left the door open.

JOSIE: But you approved of us. You made me come and live with you so it was easier for us to meet. You got me away from my daddy.

DONNA: I was afraid for you if they found out. And because you have Liam's eyes. When I woke last night I thought it was Liam who was standing there, that he'd come back. But when I saw it was you, I knew it was only because I hadn't been with him for so long I was wanting him again.

JOSIE: Don't talk to me about wanting, my body's like armour. The nerve ends are screeching under my skin. I need him back so I can stretch out again.

DONNA: How long since you've seen him?

JOSIE: Five weeks.

DONNA: I wonder does she know. (*Pause.*) Women have a way of knowing these things. I knew with my ex-husband when he was seeing somebody else. I knew the minute he put his hand on me. Once when we were in bed together a woman's name came into my head and I thought, he's not making love to me, he's making love to Margaret – I asked him afterwards, who's Margaret? He froze. He was, you see.

JOSIE: Sometimes when we make love I pretend I'm somebody else.

DONNA: Who?

JOSIE: Not someone I know. Someone I make up – from another century. Sometimes I'm not even a woman. Sometimes I'm a man – his warrior lover, fighting side by side to the death. Sometimes we're not even on the same side.

DONNA: That's powerful, Josie! (*Pause.*) What will you do if he doesn't come back?

JOSIE: Why do you say that?

DONNA: The man is still married to someone else. He has known you all these years – but he has never left his wife.

JOSIE: But she's not important to him!

DONNA: Wives are always important.

JOSIE: You only say that because you're so anxious to marry my brother.

DONNA: I must have struck home!

JOSIE: I'm sorry. (*She suddenly stops. Footsteps clattering in the alley towards the door.*) Listen.

DONNA: You've ears like a cat.

JOSIE: It's Frieda. She always walks as if her feet don't belong to her.

DONNA: Here. (*Offers her a hanky.*) Blow your nose.

(*The door bursts open.* FRIEDA *arrives, breathing deeply. Leans against the closed door.*)

FRIEDA: Oh God!

DONNA: What's wrong?

FRIEDA: I was nearly gang-raped at the club.

JOSIE: Is that all?

DONNA: Don't do that again. You gave us the fright of our lives. The way you came down that alley.

FRIEDA: I was rehearsing at the club for the Prisoners' Dependants 'do'. It was dark and there was only Danny and myself. Danny's a friend of mine, he's a musician.

DONNA: Yes. We know.

FRIEDA: I'd been singing for about an hour when I suddenly looked around and the room was full of men. There'd been one of those meetings upstairs. They must have heard my singing and come down.

JOSIE: Like a siren.

FRIEDA: I'll ignore that. Anyway, Danny sent me home. I was the only woman in the room.

JOSIE: No doubt you made the most of it.

DONNA: Strange there was a meeting and you weren't there.

JOSIE: I'm going out later.

FRIEDA: You'll never guess what I was singing when they came down to listen!

DONNA: I'll never guess.

FRIEDA: My own song. We were rehearsing a song I had written myself.

DONNA: It was that bad, was it? (*Pause.*) I'm only joking. That's great Frieda. That's a break for you.

FRIEDA: Must have been something important going on. Cathal O'Donnell was there. He stopped to talk to me on my way out. He said I'd a great voice. He had that doe-eyed look about him; you know the one – I'm married, please rescue me. I could hardly get away from him.

JOSIE: O'Donnell's in the north?

FRIEDA: I think he's been here for a while. I thought I saw him there last week as well. You know how distinctive he looks. He's so lean and dark and brooding.

DONNA: Are you going to wash your hair tonight? There's plenty of hot water.

FRIEDA: I am, then I'll do yours.

DONNA: Good. My roots are beginning to show.

FRIEDA: (*To* JOSIE) Are you all right?

DONNA: She's got a bit of a cold. Why don't you take your things and go and do your hair now.

FRIEDA: There's no rush.

DONNA: There is – I want an early night.

FRIEDA: She's just said she's got to go out.

DONNA: I still want an early night.

FRIEDA: What's wrong with you?

JOSIE: I've got earache and a sore throat; I haven't had a good night's sleep for a long time.

FRIEDA: (*Pause.*) Do you know what I thought you said? I haven't had a man to sleep with for a long time.

DONNA: Frieda! While the water's warm!

FRIEDA: I'm going. I'm going.

(FRIEDA *exits.*)

DONNA: Why don't you go and have a sleep before you go out?

JOSIE: He's here, Donna. He talked to her!

DONNA: Quick, before she comes back. Sleep in my room. Then you won't have to listen to Frieda all evening.

JOSIE: Why doesn't he come? Is it her? She says he wants her.

DONNA: Oh stop it. It's all in Frieda's mind. She doesn't know who to be at!

JOSIE: I don't know if I could share him.

DONNA: You're already sharing him! Stop tormenting yourself.

Why don't you have a wee sleep before you go out?

JOSIE: I can't, not now. I'm going to see him in a few hours.

(*In the distance the faint sound of bin lids hammering on the pavement.*)

DONNA: Bin lids.

JOSIE: Quite far off.

DONNA: Somebody's been lifted.

JOSIE: No doubt.

(*They listen again. It seems to get louder.*)

DONNA: Is it getting closer?

JOSIE: No. It's the wind. It's changed direction.

(*It stops.*)

DONNA: It makes me nervous. Nights like this. I'm glad Liam's in prison – God forgive me – it means I don't have to lie awake waiting for them to come for him. Listening to every sound. I wouldn't go through that again for anything.

(*Sound of helicopter faintly in the background.*)

JOSIE: My mother spent her life listening. My father was picked up four times.

DONNA: Oh, I hope they're not going to raid us. I only got the carpets down at Christmas. I'll never get the doors to close. That happened the last time they came. They pulled up the carpets and half the floorboards. That was after your brother'd been arrested, and I'd no one to help me put them back.

(*Bin lids begin faintly again.* FRIEDA *opens the door. She is wearing a tinfoil turban.*)

FRIEDA: Well, girls, what do you think – Miss Andersonstown second year running.

(JOSIE *motions her to be quiet. She listens.*)

What is it, a raid? It's far enough away. (*They all listen.*) Do you remember the last time you were raided?

DONNA: I was just talking about that.

FRIEDA: It was hardly worth their while. They only found a couple of rounds of ammunition. I remember this place the morning after, though. It was a shambles.

DONNA: Don't remind me.

(*The bin lids die.*)

JOSIE: It's stopped.

DONNA: I wish you didn't have to go out again tonight.

FRIEDA: I must say you don't look very well.

JOSIE: I don't look well?

DONNA: (*Eyeing* FRIEDA *also*) What's the tinfoil for?

FRIEDA: They use tinfoil at the salon, I'll be blonde in ten minutes.

DONNA: Why do hairdressers think they always have to be blonde!

FRIEDA: It's not that. It's for my act. Marlene Dietrich was blonde.

JOSIE: If you spent as much time on your mind as you do on your appearance you'd be better equipped.

FRIEDA: For what? I want to be a singer, not an academic.

JOSIE: A few exam passes might help.

FRIEDA: How did it help you? You went to university, but you still live in Andersonstown.

JOSIE: I live here because I choose to.

FRIEDA: I don't believe you – anyway, Marilyn Monroe didn't pass any exams.

(DONNA *and* JOSIE *laugh.*)

DONNA: What did I tell you? Monroe! Dietrich! She's a head about herself.

JOSIE: Why do you always want to be somebody else?

FRIEDA: I don't always want to be somebody else. I just want to be somebody.

JOSIE: Be yourself.

FRIEDA: When did I ever have a chance to be myself? My father was interned before I was born. My brother's in the Kesh for bank robbery. You mention the name McCoy in this neighbourhood, people start walking away from you backwards. I'm fed up living here, this place is a hole!

JOSIE: If it's a hole, it's a hole for all of us.

FRIEDA: Yeah, but there's this voice in my head which says – 'Nobody knows you. Nobody knows you exist. You've got to make yourself known.'

JOSIE: Is that why you've attached yourself to the Workers' Party?

DONNA: Have you?

JOSIE: She was seen with them at a dance at Queen's last week.

FRIEDA: I was talking to John McDermot.

JOSIE: You were also seen coming out of Maguire's pub on Saturday.

FRIEDA: I thought that was Gabriel driving off when I waved.

JOSIE: Maguire's is where the Officials hang out.

FRIEDA: You ought to apply to the SAS, Josie. They could use somebody with your intelligence.

JOSIE: You may be my sister, but it won't save you! You're in and out of the Club all the time. You could be carrying information to the Officials.

FRIEDA: I've nothing to do with the Officials. I was talking to John McDermot.

JOSIE: I know you wouldn't talk; but there's others who might point the finger at you. You'll put all of us under suspicion.

DONNA: Josie's right. They're paranoid about informers now. You'll get your family a bad name.

FRIEDA: Could we sink any lower?

JOSIE: I give up with you. Liam's getting out of the Kesh next month; talk to him about it.

FRIEDA: I don't know why you're making such a fuss. John McDermot is an old friend. You used to like him yourself when he was Liam's mate.

JOSIE: Not these days, my girl. The only loyalties you are allowed are ideological.

FRIEDA: Baloney! Look at her! She's not living with an ideology. My brother's changed his political line three times at least since 'sixty-nine. He joined the Officials when they split with the Provos, then the INLA when they split from the Officials; the last time he was out on parole he was impersonating votes for the Sinn Fein election. And I hear lately while he's in the Kesh he's joined the Provos! Now what does that tell us – apart from the fact that he's a relentless political opportunist?

JOSIE: Liam's always been confused!

FRIEDA: Wrong answer. The Provos are big in this area. My daddy's a big fella in the Provos, so when the son gets out after five years inside, guess who's the young pretender? Meanwhile, she still writes her twenty-two page letters to him every night and has done since the beginning. Not that he's worth it, but you have to admire her tenacity for sticking with him. That's the only loyalty I know or care about. Loyalty to someone you love, regardless! I'd like to think if I loved someone I'd follow that person to hell! Politics has nothing to do with it!

JOSIE: One day you will understand, when you come to the limits of what you can do by yourself, that this is not dogma, that there are no personal differences between one person and another that are not political.

FRIEDA: You can't believe that.

JOSIE: I do. I do.

DONNA: I wish you two would give over. You're like chalk and cheese, you always have been.

JOSIE: Do you know what they did when they divided this country –

FRIEDA: Oh, here we go again. Mystical alienation.

JOSIE: They gave us political amnesia.

FRIEDA: Jargon.

DONNA: (*Getting up*) Would anyone like a drink? I'm going to open a bottle.

FRIEDA: Do you mean to tell me you've got booze in this house?

DONNA: Did you get me any sugar?

FRIEDA: (*Waves her hand.*) Oh, apart from the Château Lenadoon.

DONNA: (*Hurt*) What's wrong with it?

FRIEDA: I think the French do it better.

DONNA: Do you not want any?

FRIEDA: I will if there's nothing else.

DONNA: Will you have a drink, Josie? It'll relax you?

JOSIE: I shouldn't.

DONNA: (*Disappearing to the kitchen*) I'll bring three glasses.

FRIEDA: When does Liam actually get out?
JOSIE: Two weeks.
FRIEDA: What will you do? Stay on here?
JOSIE: No. Probably move back to my daddy's.
FRIEDA: After all this time? You'll enjoy that.
JOSIE: I don't see any alternative.
FRIEDA: I'm glad it's not me. I wouldn't want to be his housekeeper.
JOSIE: It's purely economic.
FRIEDA: Oh, now. We never do anything we don't want to do.
JOSIE: But we do! Often.
DONNA: (*Returning*) It looks a bit cloudy, but I expect it'll settle.
FRIEDA: When do you want me to do your hair?
DONNA: I've changed my mind.
FRIEDA: Why?
DONNA: If I go up to the prison tomorrow with dyed hair Liam'll think I'm running after somebody.
FRIEDA: So what?
DONNA: So it's not worth the fights.
FRIEDA: That's ridiculous.

(*Doorbell*)

JOSIE: Who's that at this time?

(DONNA *moves cautiously to look out of the window. She turns out the light and pulls back the curtain, rattling the venetian blind as she looks out without being seen from the outside.*)

DONNA: It's two men. Jesus Christ! It's your daddy!

(*She switches the light on again.* JOSIE *lifts the bottle and glasses and runs into the kitchen.* FRIEDA *does not move. The doorbell rings again as* JOSIE *returns.*)

What'll I do?

JOSIE: Wait a minute. (*To* FRIEDA) Get rid of that ashtray! And open the back door.
FRIEDA: (*Unmoved*) What for?
JOSIE: To let fresh air in.
FRIEDA: The whole place stinks. He'll know.

(*Doorbell, more urgently*)

JOSIE: (*To* DONNA) All right, open it.

(DONNA *exits to open the front door.* JOSIE *rushes into the kitchen with the three glasses and the bottle of wine, while* FRIEDA *refuses to co-operate.*)

FRIEDA: What are you tidying up for? Why don't you be yourself?

(DONNA *lets two men quickly into the room. One of them is* MALACHY MCCOY, *Josie's and Frieda's father. The other is a younger man whom the women have never seen before.*)

MALACHY: (*Reacting to the smoke-filled room; he waves his arm in front of his face.*) In the name a'Jesus! Is this how you spend your time? Who's been smoking in here?

FRIEDA: I have!

MALACHY: Oh yes. (*Coughing violently*) It would be you. You think because you're living round at your auntie's you can do what you like. I'll bring you home one of these days if you're not careful.

FRIEDA: Suits me. I wouldn't have to look after them.

MALACHY: What have you got on your head?

FRIEDA: Tinfoil.

MALACHY: I can see that! (JOSIE *returns, he puts his arm round her to draw her near in a bear hug.*) How's my mate! Hey!

JOSIE: (*Resisting the embrace*) I'm not your mate. I'm your daughter.

MALACHY: (*Angry, releasing her from his grip*) Jesus Christ! What's wrong with you, for God's sake!

FRIEDA: (*Sweetly, to* JOE) Don't mind our father. It's just that we don't have a mother any more and he's kinda protective.

MALACHY: That's enough from you.

FRIEDA: Well, are you going to introduce us or do we have to do it ourselves?

MALACHY: This is Joe Conran.

JOE: Hello.

MALACHY: My daughter, Josie.

JOSIE: Hello.

MALACHY: (*Coughs.*) This is Donna, my son's wife.

DONNA: Hello Joe.

MALACHY: And that creature in the tinfoil – for whatever reason – is my other daughter, Frieda.

FRIEDA: Hello Joe Conran.

MALACHY: Joe's going to stop here for a while. Maybe a couple of nights or so.

JOSIE: I wasn't expecting you.

MALACHY: We weren't expecting to be raided at the top end of the estate.

JOSIE: Oh, I see.

MALACHY: Did you not hear them?

JOSIE: Yes, earlier.

MALACHY: What a night. I don't know where they're getting their information from. This is probably the safest place. He's in your care – from now on.

JOSIE: I see.

MALACHY: (*To* DONNA *and* FRIEDA) You're not to go asking him any questions about what he's doing here. Do you hear me, Frieda?

(*She feigns surprise.*)

(*To* JOE) And you're not to answer any questions until the time comes. She's a mouth like the QE2. Josie's responsible for you.

JOE: Fine.

DONNA: Where's he going to sleep?

MALACHY: He can sleep down here on the sofa. Sure, it's only for an odd night.

JOSIE: No, he can't do that. He can have my bed. (FRIEDA *is looking wide-eyed at* JOSIE. JOSIE *ignores her.*) He probably needs his sleep. I'll sleep down here.

JOE: Oh, no, I couldn't – I'm used to sleeping – anywhere – and this is very nice. I couldn't put you out.

JOSIE: You're not putting me out.

MALACHY: Well, sort it out between you. I'll be on my way.

(*To* JOSIE, *taking her aside*) You know what your instructions are. (JOSIE *nods.*)

Liam will be out soon . . . you'll be coming home . . . I'll get your room painted.

JOSIE: We'll see.

MALACHY: I'll be glad to have him back – the business is too much for one.

DONNA: Sure I thought Gabriel was helping you.

MALACHY: Gabriel nearly ruined me. He paints everything that moves. A woman rang me up the other day – he'd painted all her windows shut. Nobody paints gloss like Liam.

DONNA: Would you like a cup of tea before you go?

MALACHY: No thanks, I'd better be getting back. (*He turns to go.*)

FRIEDA: Daddy! Will you be at the Prisoners' Dependants 'do'?

MALACHY: Why?

FRIEDA: I'm singing one of my own compositions.

MALACHY: I don't know. I'll see. Wait a minute. (*Puts his hand into his pocket.*) Here's a couple of quid. Buy yourselves a bar of chocolate.

JOSIE: Thanks, Daddy.

DONNA: Cheerio, Mr McCoy.

FRIEDA: Goodbye, Father. (MALACHY *exits.*) Chocolates! Sweeties! What age does he think we are! A bottle of whiskey would be more like it.

JOE: I have one in my travelling bag. I got it on the boat. (*He puts his bag on the floor.*)

FRIEDA: (*Full of admiration*) Good man!

JOSIE: (*Restraining* JOE *from opening his bag.*) I suggest you keep it in your bag. My sister and a glass of whiskey are quite a combination.

FRIEDA: Am I? That's the nicest thing you've said about me all evening.

JOSIE: The grain and the grape don't mix. Your wine's in the kitchen.

DONNA: (*To* JOE) Would you like a cuppa tea, Joe?

JOE: I don't drink tea.

DONNA: You're joking.

JOE: No, I'm not.

DONNA: Coffee?

JOE: Yes, that would be lovely.

DONNA: Right.
FRIEDA: Why do you not drink tea?
DONNA: Frieda!
FRIEDA: No, I'm interested. Do you not like it?
JOE: No.
FRIEDA: Did something happen to put you off it?
JOE: When I was at school I had to drink tea and I didn't like it, so I've never drunk it since.
FRIEDA: When you were at school?
DONNA: Was that like a boarding school?
JOE: Public school, yes.
FRIEDA: What public school did you go to?
JOE: I went to Ampleforth.

(DONNA *and* FRIEDA *can hardly suppress their disbelief. Only* JOSIE *appears uninterested and even impatient.*)

DONNA: Well, if you'll excuse me for a minute I'll just get you a cup of coffee.

(*She exits.* FRIEDA *sits down beside* JOE.)

JOSIE: Your wine's in the kitchen.
FRIEDA: Donna'll bring it out when she's coming.
JOSIE: We've got some homemade wine, would you like some?
JOE: No, thank you.
FRIEDA: You don't like wine either?
JOE: No, I do, very much. But I prefer to leave it to the experts.
FRIEDA: That's just what I said.
JOE: Would you like a cigarette, Frieda? You smoke, don't you?
FRIEDA: Listen, we all do, but these two are so afraid of my da they won't admit it.
JOE: (*Laughs.*) Oh, I see. Well, help yourselves.

(*They take the packet.*)

Do you live here as well?

FRIEDA: No, I live round the corner.
JOE: You're a singer?
FRIEDA: You've heard about me?
JOE: You told your father you were singing one of your own compositions.
FRIEDA: I'm a singer/songwriter.

JOSIE: She works in the hairdresser's by the bus depot.

FRIEDA: I still sing.

DONNA: (*Opening the kitchen door*) Do you like it made with milk or water?

JOE: I like it black, thanks.

DONNA: (*To herself*) Black. (*Withdrawing again*)

JOE: Is that what you want to be, a professional singer?

FRIEDA: Och, no – that's only a front. What I really want is to marry somebody rich and live abroad.

JOE: I'm not exactly sure when you're serious and when you're joking.

FRIEDA: Oh, I'm perfectly serious. Do you think I want to end up like my big sister here? Running about like a wee messenger girl for my father and his cronies. No thanks. And if she's not careful she'll finish up like my auntie Cora. Do you know about my father's maiden sisters?

JOE: No.

FRIEDA: I live with them. Cora is blind and deaf and dumb and she has no hands, and she's been like that since she was eighteen. And Bridget, the other one, is a maid because she stayed to look after Cora. And I'm still a maid because I'm looking after both of them.

JOE: What happened to your aunt when she was eighteen?

FRIEDA: Oh, the usual. She was storing ammunition for her wee brother Malachy – my father, God love him – who was in the IRA even then. He asked her to move it. Unfortunately it was in poor condition, technically what you call weeping. So when she pulled up the floorboards in her bedroom – whoosh! It took the skin off her face. Her hair's never really grown properly since and look – no hands! (*She demonstrates by pulling her fists up into her sleeves.* DONNA *comes into the room with coffee for* JOE.)

DONNA: God forgive you! (*To* JOE) I hope this is all right.

FRIEDA: They stick her out at the front of the parades every so often to show the women of Ireland what their patriotic duty should be. But I'll tell you something – it won't be mine!

JOSIE: She was supposed to have been a beautiful girl, my auntie Cora. My father told me that. So I suppose you could say she really had something to sacrifice.

DONNA: We've all got something to sacrifice!

FRIEDA: You're right! And when there's a tricolour over the City Hall, Donna will still be making coffee for Joe Conran, and Josie will still be keeping house for her daddy, because it doesn't matter a damn whether the British are here or not.

JOSIE: That's just your excuse for not doing anything.

FRIEDA: Aye. But it's a good one. (*To* JOE) So, Joe Conran, now that you know about us, what are you doing here?

JOE: (*Looking to* JOSIE, *who gives him no help whatsoever*) I'm not supposed to answer any questions.

FRIEDA: Oh come on, this is family.

JOE: My grandfather was Irish. He married a Catholic. My grandmother, Teresa Conran, was a friend of Connolly's.

DONNA: James Connolly?

FRIEDA: You're here because your granny knew Connolly? (*Pause.*) She didn't meet him at the parents' association at Eton, did she?

JOSIE: Frieda?

FRIEDA: What?

JOSIE: How long did you say you had to keep the tinfoil on for?

FRIEDA: (*Touches her head.*) Oh fuck! Ten minutes! (*Dashes out and slams the door.*)

DONNA: I think I'd better help her with the head dress. (*She exits.*)

JOE: So you're the courier?
(JOSIE *nods.*)
What exactly do you do?

JOSIE: I take messages between the commanders, move the stuff from one place to another, or people. I operate at nights mostly, which is why I was offering you my bed. I'm hardly ever in it.

JOE: Your security's not very good on this estate. I'd only just arrived when the Army came up the road. Why did that happen?

JOSIE: There've been a lot of raids recently. Informers using the confidential telephones – it's always the same after a bombing campaign.

JOE: Are the others involved? (*Indicates the kitchen.*)

JOSIE: Donna has a child to look after.

JOE: And Frieda?

JOSIE: Well, you've seen her.

JOE: Can they be trusted?

JOSIE: This is family.

JOE: You must be very brave.

JOSIE: I'm not brave. I just began doing this before I had to think of the consequences. I think I'm more scared than I was ten years ago. But I'm getting better at smiling at soldiers. (*She smiles at him.*)

JOE: You shouldn't do that.

JOSIE: What?

JOE: Smile at soldiers.

JOSIE: Why not?

JOE: If you smile to deceive, how will I know when it's for real?

JOSIE: (*Laughs.*) I think that's the least of your worries.

JOE: Worries? Do I have worries?

JOSIE: Now humour I didn't expect.

JOE: What did you expect?

(*She gets up.*)

JOSIE: I have to go out for a while.

JOE: Are you married, Josie?

JOSIE: (*Putting on her coat*) No.

JOE: Do you have a boyfriend?

JOSIE: You ask too many questions, Joe Conran.

JOE: I know, but you have such beautiful eyes I can't help wondering.

JOSIE: I'm very puritanical. I wanted to be a nun once – and you're not going to charm your way into this organization.

JOE: Charm? I was interrogated in Amsterdam!

JOSIE: You weren't interrogated, you were questioned. There are still some questions you need to answer before we're satisfied.

JOE: But how long, how long am I going to be here?

JOSIE: For a while.

JOE: So I'm not going to meet anyone tonight?

JOSIE: No. You're going to stay here with me for a while.
(*Frieda's voice offstage from the kitchen, singing:*
'Oh love is pleasing and love is teasing and love is – ')
I suggest you go to bed soon. Then you won't have to tell any more lies. Eton? You surprise me.
(JOSIE *exits by the front door.* JOE *sits down. The singing stops as* FRIEDA *enters the room carrying a glass in each hand. She has a towel around her head like a turban and she is dressed only in a long towelling dressing-gown, which is tied at the waist.* JOE *pays no attention to her entrance until she speaks.*)

FRIEDA: I'm sorry I was so long.
(*She puts the empty glasses down, and begins to rummage through Joe's travelling bag.*)

JOE: What are you doing?

FRIEDA: You said you had whiskey. I'm looking for it. (*She takes the bottle out.*) Would you like a glass?

JOE: Thanks. (*She pours whiskey.*)

FRIEDA: Would you have a cigarette?

JOE: I think you have the packet.

FRIEDA: Oh, so I have.
(*She sits down on the sofa beside him.* JOE *remains obstinately preoccupied, and looking around the room.*)

JOE: I wanted to ask you something.

FRIEDA: Yes?

JOE: Why are you so critical of your family's involvement with the Republican movement?

FRIEDA: Oh, I wouldn't say I was critical exactly. I mean, I respect them all very much. My father's a great man and Josie's so committed. You have to admire her and Liam's dedication. I mean, what the Brits have done to my family would make you weep.

JOE: But you're not an activist?

FRIEDA: No. Well, I used to be. I gave all that up in the seventies. God, I was on more demonstrations than enough.

JOE: So you're not political at all now?

FRIEDA: Well, that's not true either. I sing.

JOE: You sing?

FRIEDA: Yes. That's what I do instead. (*She gets up as she is speaking and walks around the room, finally turning to face him.*) Can you see my pubic hair?

JOE: No.

FRIEDA: Oh good. I was a bit worried in case you could. I'm anti-nationalist, that's all.

JOE: What do you mean by that?

FRIEDA: Nationalism is always the last resort of people who've failed to achieve anything else. Joe, could we be friends? (*Sits down beside him again, very close.*)

JOE: Well, I wouldn't want to argue with you, Frieda.

FRIEDA: Oh, but I love arguing. Before Donna comes in, there's something I've been wanting to tell you – you're disturbing me and I'd like to do something about it. Since you walked in here tonight I thought – yes, him! Let me see your hand. (*She grabs his hand.*) Are you a Scorpio?

JOE: I'm very easily seduced. I'm on a job here – I don't want to get involved.

(DONNA *comes in from the kitchen. She has a towel over her shoulders, she has just washed her hair.*)

DONNA: I see you've opened the whiskey, Frieda.

(JOE *gets up.*)

JOE: Can you tell me where you want me to sleep?

DONNA: Oh yes, of course. I'm sorry. I should have said so earlier. Josie's room at the top of the stairs.

JOE: Thank you. Goodnight.

DONNA: What about your whiskey?

JOE: Please help yourselves. Goodnight.

(*He leaves the room. Footsteps heard on the stairs.*)

DONNA: Do you have to throw yourself at every man on the run who stays under my roof! What do you think this place is?

FRIEDA: What's wrong, did I get to him first?

DONNA: You watch your tongue!

FRIEDA: You never object to Josie doing it. She threw herself at him as soon as he arrived. He's sleeping in her bed for God's sake. Don't think I don't know why Josie stays here, and not at home with my father. Helping you with Catherine. My God, I've never seen any evidence of it.

DONNA: Josie, whatever she does, is older than you are.

FRIEDA: Josie's older than any of us.

DONNA: That may well be . . .

FRIEDA: At least four hundred years! (FRIEDA *begins to cry.*)

DONNA: You shouldn't drink. Whiskey always makes you cry.

FRIEDA: Nobody seems to care what happens to me. If I died tomorrow – it would be no loss.

DONNA: I care, Frieda.

FRIEDA: Oh yes, I know, but I was talking about love!

DONNA: I love you, Frieda.

FRIEDA: Yes, I know, but I want to be happy with someone! I haven't anyone of my own. Sometimes when I'm walking along the street and I see a couple holding hands I have to look away – I'm so jealous. Other times I look closely at the woman and think, well, I'm more attractive than her, why doesn't that man notice me? And lots of times I just wander around looking at men.

DONNA: Happiness requires all your intelligence. You won't find it just by looking; and the only thing you'll get from a man who looks like Joe Conran is a lot of trouble. But that's only my opinion. You must make up your own mind.

FRIEDA: (*Sniffing*) No. It's all right. I don't fancy him, anyway. I think he's got sexual problems.

DONNA: (*Putting the top on the whiskey bottle*) Oh well, that's all right then. Let's have a look at this hair of yours and see how well it's taken.

FRIEDA: No, wait. I have to dry it first.

(FRIEDA *exits.*)

SCENE 3

DONNA, JOSIE.

Several hours later. DONNA *is in bed. A cot stands beside the bed, and a night light by the cot. Slowly the door opens in the dark and light falls across the room. A figure is silhouetted in the doorway; the figure approaches the cot.* DONNA *turns instinctively as the figure approaches.*

DONNA: Who's there?
(*The baby murmurs.*)
Please don't wake her.
JOSIE: It's all right, she's looking for us.
DONNA: What did you say?
JOSIE: She's looking through her life for us. She'll be back in a minute.
(DONNA *gets out of bed quickly and takes* JOSIE*'s arm.*)
DONNA: Wake up, Josie. Wake up.
JOSIE: Oh. Oh. (*Shivering*) I'm very cold.
DONNA: Come to bed.
(DONNA *helps her into bed.*)
Here, I'll make a bucket with my nightdress. It's better than the sofa . . . Do you remember when we were kids we used to do this. You, me and Frieda in a double bed. We all had to face in the same direction or we wouldn't fit in. Except Frieda kept turning the other way and we had to push her out. She'd run off crying to your mammy and we'd to bribe her to keep her quiet . . . What's wrong? Was he not at the meeting?
JOSIE: He knew I was going to be there, but he didn't wait!
DONNA: You're shivering, hold on to me.
JOSIE: He left before I arrived, Donna. Half an hour. He's in this town, he talked to Frieda tonight, but he wouldn't wait for me!
DONNA: Don't abandon yourself like this!
JOSIE: He told me I invaded his life.
DONNA: Invaded. It's not a word I would use.
JOSIE: Oh, Donna, I did make him happy. I did!
DONNA: I know, love. I know.

SCENE 4

FRIEDA, DANNY, MCDERMOT, MALACHY, GABRIEL, SECOND MAN.

FRIEDA *is sitting on a high stool in a circle of light. The setting is the club. Hanging down from the walls behind her are portraits of the ten dead hunger strikers, visible now that the lights are on. Frieda's song is accompanied by* DANNY *at the piano.*

FRIEDA:

When I was young my father
Walked me through the hall to see
Where Connolly, Pearse and Plunkett hung;
A profile against the darkening sky
My father pointed out to me,
Was the greatest name of all,
To be called the Volunteer,
To be called the Volunteer.

When I grew up my first love
Whispered in my ear,
What do you most desire, my love?
What do you most desire?
Lying on a moonlit beach
I held his hand and said
To be a Volunteer, my love,
To be a Volunteer.

(*Someone is whistling.* DANNY *stops, addressing a young man in the darkness.*)

DANNY: I'm sorry, you can't come in. We're not open till seven. This is a rehearsal.

MCDERMOT: It's not a rehearsal she needs; it's an education!

FRIEDA: (*Covering her eyes from the lights and peering out into the darkness*) Who is that?

MCDERMOT: I came to see what you did in your spare time.

FRIEDA: John McDermot, have you gone mad!

DANNY: Do you know him?

FRIEDA: Could we take a break now?

MCDERMOT: Come back in a hundred years: she needs all the time she can get!

FRIEDA: Go on. (*Pushing the hesitant* DANNY *out*) It's all right. He really is a friend of mine. (DANNY *exits*.) Why do your jokes always sound like a threat?

MCDERMOT: You think I was joking?

FRIEDA: What are you doing here anyway?

MCDERMOT: You were supposed to be selling papers with me on Saturday. What happened to you?

FRIEDA: You're mad coming in here!

MCDERMOT: What did you do to your hair? Is that a disguise so I wouldn't ever recognize you again!

FRIEDA: Oh, don't you start.

MCDERMOT: On second thoughts, it's just as well you didn't come out on Saturday. I would have had to explain that your appearance was your own idea and in no way reflected the views of the Workers' Party.

FRIEDA: It's for my act.

MCDERMOT: The song you were singing, was that part of your act as well?

FRIEDA: Before you say anything devastating, I wrote that song.

MCDERMOT: I thought you did. (*Pause*.) Do you want to know what I think?

FRIEDA: (*Puts her hands over her ears*.) I don't want to hear. I never listen to criticism.

(FRIEDA *has her hands over her ears and she is humming. He pulls her hands away*.)

MCDERMOT: Listen, you! It's about time you came out of the closet and stood up for what you believe in. Instead of singing these endless Republican dirges around the clubs! 'The greatest name of all, to be a Volunteer'!

FRIEDA: I wrote it after Bobby Sands died. It's very popular here, you know. It's always requested.

MCDERMOT: Listen, kid. You want to be big? You want to lead the tribe, not follow it. This song celebrates militarism. How many times have you been told it's the Party not the

Army that is dominant. The political thinker, not the soldier. That's the greatest name of all. You know that – you've known it since you were seventeen. You must use everything you know when you write songs, Frieda.

FRIEDA: There haven't been many moments in my life when I've felt honest; the feeling I had when I wrote that song was one of them. When I feel I can write a song about the Party I'll let you know.

MCDERMOT: He who suffers the most! That's you all over. You weep at Bobby Sands's funeral, but a bomb in a store and the IRA are bastards. You could end up on both sides of the border if you don't think!

FRIEDA: At least I'd see everybody's point of view.

MCDERMOT: If you can see everybody's point of view you can see nothing at all. What you lack is a conceptual framework.

FRIEDA: One of these days, John McDermot, you'll collapse in a conceptual framework.

(*A door bangs.* GABRIEL *appears.*)

GABRIEL: You're a bit out of your territory, fella.

MCDERMOT: And you're out of your depth – son.

FRIEDA: Look, Gabriel, we don't want any trouble. He's with me. We were just leaving.

GABRIEL: My uncle Malachy won't like it when he hears about this.

FRIEDA: He can say what he likes, I've never been afraid of my father. I'm not about to start because he's drilling the Boy Scouts!

GABRIEL: You can tell him that yourself. (*Door bangs.*) Here he is now.

(MALACHY *comes in, followed by the* SECOND MAN.)

FRIEDA: Oh fuck!

(FRIEDA *takes John's arm and braces herself to confront* MALACHY.)

MALACHY: What's he doing here?

FRIEDA: He's with me.

MALACHY: Get him out of here!

FRIEDA: No, no. Wait!

(MCDERMOT *and* FRIEDA *are dragged apart.*)

SECOND MAN: Have you no control over your daughter?

(MCDERMOT *is pushed roughly towards the door by* GABRIEL *and the* SECOND MAN. *They exit.* MALACHY *has caught* FRIEDA *by the wrist to restrain her from following. He now pushes her across the room.*)

MALACHY: You stay – (FRIEDA *is struck on the back of the head by* MALACHY.) – away from him!

(FRIEDA *remains holding her head, momentarily stunned.*)

You'll not make a little boy of me! I'm sick to death of hearing about you . . . All I get is complaints . . . bringing that hood in here.

FRIEDA: (*Recovering*) What do I have to do or say, Father, to get you to leave me alone –

MALACHY: I'll leave you alone all right. I'll leave you so you'll wish you'd never been born.

(*He makes a race at her. She pushes a table into his path.*)

FRIEDA: Oh, Mammy. Mammy.

(*He attempts to punch her in the stomach.*)

MALACHY: You'll not make little of me. Siding with the people who condemned Bobby Sands.

FRIEDA: (*Backing away towards the door*) They didn't condemn him. They said he beat his wife! Hard to believe, isn't it?

MALACHY: Get out of my sight.

(*Overturned club furniture stands between them.*)

FRIEDA: They say when he was dying she was so afraid of him she wouldn't go up to the prison to see him. In fact she wouldn't go near him until she was sure he was definitely dead.

MALACHY: Never let me see your face again.

FRIEDA: (*Still backing out*) You know something, Father? You've been burying your friends since 'sixty-nine. But do you know something else, your friends have been burying you!

MALACHY: Never cross my door again!

FRIEDA: (*Desperation*) We are the dying. Why are we mourning them! (*She points at the portraits of the dead hunger strikers. She exits.*)

SCENE 5

DANNY, GABRIEL, SECOND MAN, MCDERMOT, FRIEDA.
Outside the club, at the back, JOHN MCDERMOT *is on the ground trying to protect his ribs and head from the feet of his two attackers.* DANNY *comes rushing in on them.*

DANNY: For Christ's sake, are yous mad?
GABRIEL: What's wrong with you, McLoughlin!
DANNY: There's a foot patrol at the top of the entry – you can hear yous a mile away.
GABRIEL: Beat it!
(*The* TWO MEN *run off,* DANNY *appears to follow, then stops and returns to* MCDERMOT.)
DANNY: Are you OK?
MCDERMOT: (*Beginning to look for his glasses*) I don't know yet. I can't see a thing.
DANNY: (*Stoops to retrieve them.*) I'm afraid they're broken.
MCDERMOT: (*Taking them from him*) Oh shit. I have another pair but – they're not as good. (*He tries to fix them.*) I hope I can remember where I put them.
DANNY: I don't know who you are or where you're coming from but next time they'll kill you . . .
(MCDERMOT *doesn't reply.*)
Is she worth it?
MCDERMOT: Did you say the Army were about?
DANNY: Aye, for their benefit.
(FRIEDA*'s footsteps are heard coming towards them.*)
FRIEDA: Where's John McDermot?
DANNY: Hey, Frieda! Over here! He's OK, calm down! He'll live.
FRIEDA: (*Gets down on her knees to face* JOHN, *who is propped against the wall.*) You stupid, thoughtless, reckless, insensitive, selfish bastard!

DANNY: Aye, well, I'll head away on.

FRIEDA: I could murder you! You have blown my one chance! Walking in there tonight and brazenly exhibiting yourself.

DANNY: I wouldn't hang about. Those boys might come back. (DANNY *exits.*)

MCDERMOT: You didn't have to say you were with me.

FRIEDA: Who did you come to talk to – my daddy?

MCDERMOT: I'm sorry.

FRIEDA: (*Getting to her feet*) Well, you're responsible for me now.

MCDERMOT: Don't be silly. Nobody's responsible for you . . . Are you all right?

FRIEDA: No, I'm not. My head aches and my stomach's heaving – I think I'm going to be sick.

MCDERMOT: It's the shock!

FRIEDA: Shock? My life's in ruins. My father thinks I'm in the Workers' Party, and he thinks you and I are lovers. Jesus, when our Liam gets out of the Kesh he'll probably kill both of us.

MCDERMOT: What do you want to do about it?

FRIEDA: I've made a decision.

MCDERMOT: What's that?

FRIEDA: I'd like to join the Party.

MCDERMOT: That's a step in the right direction.

FRIEDA: It's a beginning.

MCDERMOT: Why?

FRIEDA: I have never in my life forgiven anyone who raised their hand to me.

MCDERMOT: I'll try to remember.

FRIEDA: I have another problem. I'm homeless and I don't have any money. Do you think you could find me somewhere to live?

MCDERMOT: I could take in a lodger.

FRIEDA: This is serious.

MCDERMOT: I am serious.

FRIEDA: Would your wife not mind?

MCDERMOT: We separated six months ago.

FRIEDA: In that case, no, I think not. Surely some other member of the Party could help me.

MCDERMOT: There's someone who visits me from time to time. Between you and me would be a business arrangement. I'm hardly ever at home.

FRIEDA: All right. I accept. The other thing is – I really don't have any money at the moment. I packed in my job at the hairdresser's.

MCDERMOT: I think that was wise.

FRIEDA: I want to devote more time to writing songs.

MCDERMOT: Well, I wouldn't depend on making a living from your singing career just yet, Frieda.

FRIEDA: You think not.

MCDERMOT: Your material isn't very commercial.

FRIEDA: I'm trying to get a gig at the Orpheus – or somewhere.

MCDERMOT: Well, I can't do anything about that – but we can come to some arrangement about the money when you've got some. (*Begins to try to struggle to his feet.*) Now, would you like to help me up from here. My back's killing me.

FRIEDA: (*Helping him with her arm*) Why are you doing this?

MCDERMOT: (*In some pain*) Because someone put his boot in my rib cage.

FRIEDA: No. Why are you helping me?

MCDERMOT: Because you're lost, Frieda. You're lost and I'm half blind.

FRIEDA: (*Going off with him*) I'm not lost! I just don't want all those people on my side. Do you?

SCENE 6

JOE, JOSIE, O'DONNELL, MALACHY.

The Club. In addition to the portraits of the hunger strikers there are balloons and decorations around the room. It is after closing time and the chairs are upturned on the table tops. JOE *follows* JOSIE *into the room. She switches on a small light above a table and lifts down two chairs, standing them upright on the floor.*

JOE: (*Looking around*) This is very festive.

JOSIE: It's our club. My brother's getting out tomorrow and there's to be a party.

JOE: How long's he been away?

JOSIE: Five years.

JOE: The baby's nearly two?

JOSIE: Parole. He gets out on parole.

JOE: And in between she waits?

JOSIE: Of course she waits.

JOE: When was the last time he was out?

JOSIE: He was at the birth.

JOE: Would you wait two years for a man, Josie?

JOSIE: For the right man.

JOE: Are you waiting for the right man?

JOSIE: Sit down.

JOE: You seem nervous.

JOSIE: It's cold in here.

JOE: When do I get to meet O'Donnell?

JOSIE: When you've answered my questions.

JOE: Your questions?

JOSIE: A lot of people want to meet O'Donnell, Joe. The British don't even know what he looks like. We know that.

JOE: All right, but this is the third time I will have been questioned. Amsterdam, Dublin, and now here.

JOSIE: I promise you this will be the last.

(JOE *sits in the chair* JOSIE *has indicated. Taking a file from her shoulder bag and placing it on the table she also sits down.*)

I saw this report on you – I've been dying to meet you since I read it. (*Reads from the file.*) Educated Trinity and Cambridge. First class honours Sociology. PhD. Chairman of the Socialist Society. Revolutionary Socialist Students' Federation. Member of the European International Liberation Group . . . ardent supporter of the Basque Separatist Movement . . . recently brought a group of left-wing German students into talks with the Free Wales Army on anti-technology in industry, or how to prevent, by force if necessary, the replacement of workers by machines. Also set up discussions between the Italian Communist-controlled administrations of several states and the British Left – including some of our people in Britain – on advantages of the local state. Items on the agenda: the control of police, Army and security systems, also the subsidization of communes. You're a clever fellow. Oh, and something else. You've got a very interesting emotional life. Married: 1971. Several girlfriends. Currently: in Spain, a Basque lawyer; in Germany, Hamburg, a Marxist psychoanalyst; in Italy, a dancer, or was it an actress with a socialist theatre company, whose father is a mayor of a Communist town. Now, after all those exotic locations, what brings you to West Belfast?

JOE: You make me sound like a tourist. I do take my politics home with me. (*Pause.*) My wife's an Irish Catholic.

JOSIE: I wouldn't cite loyalty to your wife as a reason for your being here – it's not exactly your most stable characteristic.

JOE: We have an arrangement.

JOSIE: That's very nice. But it doesn't answer my question.

JOE: What exactly do you want to know?

JOSIE: Let me tell you a story, Joe. When I was little my daddy used to say – 'When the British withdraw we can be human.' I believed that, since the south of Ireland was already free, there I could be human . . . Well, I'd been down south quite a few times, always to Bodenstown to the Wolfe Tone Commemorations and that meant coming back on the coach again as soon as it was over. One year when I was nearly sixteen, instead of coming straight back I stayed on and went to Dublin. I simply wanted to see the capital . . . I had no money and my shoes let in water, and I came back to Belfast at night with very wet feet in the back of a pig lorry. It smelt of pig feed. It dropped me off at seven-thirty in the morning on the Falls Road. I had time to go home and change before going to school at nine . . . There was a girl next to me in assembly. She had long straight fair hair and gleaming white teeth. If you leaned close she smelt of lemon soap. When she went to Dublin it was to buy clothes, she told me. I stood looking down at her beautifully polished shoes and I knew that it was all for her. Dublin existed for her to buy her shoes in. . . . All day the smell of pig feed stayed with me . . . From then on I stopped wanting only British withdrawal – to unite Ireland for the shoppers and the shopkeepers of Belfast and Dublin. I became a revolutionary. You see it wasn't the presence of the British that made me feel unclean that morning – it was the presence of money – Irish money as much as English money. Do you understand, Joe? What I want to know is, what are you doing in the ranks of the unhuman? I was born here.

(JOE *thinks for a minute, then reaches into his pocket, takes out his wallet, from which he quickly takes all the notes, and thrusts both wallet and notes into* JOSIE*'s hands.*)

JOE: Buy them! . . . Buy shoes! . . . You're not a revolutionary, Josie, you're a shoe fetishist. Go out, fill yourself with all the things that make you envious, then when you've got it out of your system – come back and talk to me seriously about revolution . . . You want to know what I'm doing here? It's very simple: I'm taking responsibility for what is made of me.

JOSIE: (*Puts the wallet and the money back on the table between them.*) What is made of you?

JOE: Ascendancy. Anglo-Irish. British Army. I was born there. A prisoner of circumstances you might say; circumstances which found me enrolling in Sandhurst when I was seventeen, before I could think. But I did think – so I changed. I stopped being a soldier. And I've continued to resist circumstances ever since.

JOSIE: Would you die for an impossibility?

JOE: No . . . I don't think so . . . What impossibility?

JOSIE: The thirty-two-county Workers' Republic. Connolly's dream. Some of our people, and I'm one of them, believe it to be an impossibility. A place we will never come into. But we'll die trying to get there, because I suppose this is our country and as it is our lives are meaningless . . . But your life isn't meaningless, Joe, with your international conferences and your international girl friends . . . It's hard to imagine a better life. So, come on, why are you risking so much for us? And this isn't even your country?

JOE: Not for you – for the revolution. I happen to be one of those people who believe that my government's aggression in another country has something to do with me. I also know full well that there cannot be an English revolution unless there is one in Ireland. 'A nation that enslaves another . . .'

JOSIE: '. . . can never itself be free.' You'll find that slogan on the wall behind the swimming baths. We've come a long way. Ten years ago we wouldn't have dared quote Marx on the gable walls. Now we simply don't bother to attribute it to him . . . But what would make you, with your background, support a revolution? You've too much to lose.

JOE: Absolutely. I have too much to lose. You have to trust my integrity. You put too much emphasis on the weight of experience – I am the sum of all my reading.

JOSIE: Of your reading? Do you mean books? Jesus . . . Your fucking ideas, Joe. I'm trying to find out how you actually feel. The thing is – why would you be a traitor to your own country?

JOE: I'm not a traitor – my father was an Irish Protestant son of a mixed marriage. My grandparents were Southern Unionists. My mother is an English Catholic. I was sent to Ampleforth. I went into the Army as an engineer – yes. My mother's family are all British Army. I left the Army after eighteen months and have had no connections with it since. I went back to university and read sociology and became a believer in revolutionary socialism.

JOSIE: Like many other sons of the bourgeoisie in the sixties. Fascinating generation. God I hated them. Made it all too clear to you who was in and who was out. I imagine you were in, Joe.

JOE: You seem to object to the idea that a person can refuse to render back what their social conditioning will make of them. And yet the history of the world we live in, of change and revolution, suggests we do just that very thing.

JOSIE: I'm objecting to the fact that you refuse to talk about your emotional involvement with the British.

JOE: The question of identity is very complex.

JOSIE: So it is, Joe. (*She waits while he appears to think.*) In fact it's crucial. (*Very quietly, while still awaiting his reply*) We've had a number of volunteers who come to us, usually Catholics married to Protestants, driven out of an area by loyalist intimidation. They get bitter about it and join the Republican movement to hit back. They're the worst type of volunteers as far as I'm concerned. They hit back because all they wanted was to be good Protestants, to be acceptable, like the working class who want to be middle class; blacks who want to be white. This type of volunteer hates the Protestants and the British because they are not Protestant and they are not British. They are not entirely trustworthy either because they will be among the first to back the state should conditions improve; and they will never make good revolutionaries because they are not fighting to be what they are. Until we know what you are; until you know who you are, how can we trust your motives for being here?

JOE: I didn't realize the Republican Movement was so choosey about the conscience of its recruits!

JOSIE: It's a bit like the Catholic Church, Joe; easy if you were born in it, difficult if you try to convert.

JOE: I regard myself as Irish!

JOSIE: There's no need to go that far. The thing is – are you rejecting Mother because Mother's rejecting you?

JOE: This is extraordinary.

JOSIE: You're no ordinary recruit, Joe. And it really doesn't concern us whether you regard yourself as Irish or English. You have already met on your travels a number of English socialists who work for us. If we hesitate it has nothing to do with your nationality; it is merely because we have very strong doubts about your motives.

JOE: You've said that before. What doubts?

JOSIE: Your family?

JOE: My wife's an Irish Catholic.

JOSIE: I was talking about a more binding relationship than that one – your mother's a hard woman to impress, I imagine. Was she impressed by your marriage to Rosa Connelly?

JOE: My mother's not important to me. I hardly ever see her.

JOSIE: Is that right?

JOE: She's retired to South Africa. I've never even visited her there.

JOSIE: But you do see her?

JOE: When she comes to England, yes.

JOSIE: How often? How often does she do that?

JOE: Once or twice a year.

JOSIE: Where? Where in England do you see her? At your house?

JOE: No. Rosa, my wife, doesn't – they don't get on. So my mother's never stayed with us.

JOSIE: So, when you want to see your mother, where do you see her?

JOE: Airports, restaurants, hotels.

JOSIE: And at your sister's?

JOE: My stepsister. My father died, my mother remarried.

JOSIE: Where does she live?

JOE: Sussex. But I haven't seen her for some time.

JOSIE: Christmas two years ago. Where was she living?

JOE: Sandhurst.

JOSIE: And you told us you hadn't been in touch with the Army since you bought yourself out in 1968.

JOE: It was a family matter; my mother was spending Christmas at Sandhurst with Alice.

JOSIE: And six months after that? You went back to Sandhurst but your mother wasn't there.

JOE: I had to visit Alice again. It had to do with my mother's will. I'm an executor.

JOSIE: What rank is your sister's husband?

JOE: He's a colonel.

JOSIE: Your wife was with you.

JOE: Yes, I always took her with me when I went to visit them. I don't really get on with my family and my wife has the facility to talk to anyone.

JOSIE: Except your mother?

JOE: My mother's a difficult woman.

JOSIE: And there was no difficulty with Rosa being Irish?

JOE: My father was Irish.

JOSIE: (*Appears to find this funny, but continues.*) Your wife is a Catholic from Derry.

JOE: Yes.

JOSIE: Your brother-in-law was in Derry in 'sixty-nine. The then Captain Blakemore was attached to the officer responsible there for releasing 350 CS gas canisters to the police in one night for use against the people of the Bogside – where your wife and her family lived at the time.

JOE: You can't lay that decision at the door of an Army officer. That's a political decision!

JOSIE: Not the point of my question. How did your wife get on with the Colonel, given this inconvenient piece of history?

JOE: Rosa, my wife, never talked to the Colonel. She talked to my sister. They never discussed politics.

JOSIE: What did she talk to your sister about?

JOE: Cooking.

JOSIE: Cooking?

JOE: Yes. Rosa loved cooking. Alice hated it. So Rosa did the cooking when we stayed there.

JOSIE: You say you have an arrangement with your wife. I think you mean that she left you.

JOE: We split up.

JOSIE: She left you three months after that last visit to Sandhurst.

JOE: Yes.

JOSIE: Why?

JOE: I don't know. (*Sighs.*)

JOSIE: What reason did she give you?

JOE: None. She couldn't. She didn't say anything.

(JOSIE *gets up from the table and walks to the door of the room, as if to leave.*)

JOSIE: I don't think you can realize the seriousness of the position you are in. You approached us six months ago offering us your services as a political adviser. We declined because we said we only accept that kind of advice from inside this organization. You then, as we hoped, reapplied to be an active and trained volunteer. Now, at present, as a result of our own investigations, you are under suspicion of attempting to infiltrate us as an agent of British Intelligence. If you don't deal with those suspicions, I am going to walk out of here in a few minutes' time and leave you to your fate.

JOE: But I don't know how to clear myself. You knew about my Army background. I never attempted to hide that. It was partly an asset to you.

JOSIE: Your training, yes. We knew you'd left the Army in 'sixty-eight. But what you never told us was that you visited Sandhurst Military Training Academy on several occasions in the past two years. And previously, Warminster, Bodmin and Osnabruck.

JOE: Exactly where my sister was based each time.

JOSIE: On the last occasion, eighteen months ago, after a visit to Sandhurst your wife left you. At exactly the same time Commander Kitson was also at Sandhurst. I'm sure I don't need to remind you that Kitson is head of Counter Insurgency Operations for the British Army. Now, did your wife leave you because she realized you were working for Counter Insurgency Operations? We think she did. And all you've been able to offer in reply is that your wife spent her visits to Sandhurst happily acting as a kitchen maid for the family of the man who sent CS gas into her family home in Derry.

JOE: It's not true. She was never happy about going there. She hated it. And I did too. But – I gave her no choice. She even used to cry a lot before she went. And then she'd get there and start talking to Alice. It was like a flood. The sun came out. I never knew how she did it. And because she cheered up, I thought she didn't mind in the end. I really believed everything was all right. I have not been recruited by British Intelligence. They never approached me; in fact it's been quite the opposite since I bought myself out of the Army. I met Rosa, as you know, while I was at university in Dublin. My family never approved of my going back to Ireland. My mother saw it as a rejection of her in going there and leaving the Army as I did. She actually complained once to my sister that I married Rosa to spite her, to make her ashamed. A wee hussy from the Bogside, she called her. In marrying Rosa I was also a security risk. My sister even suggested to me that her husband would probably never be made a colonel because of my connections with the wrong side in the Irish War. Not one member of my family came to the wedding. The Army of course refused permission to the Blakemores to attend, something to do with Rosa's part in the Bogside Riots of 'sixty-nine. She was a member of the Citizens' Defence Committee and her name was on the list of conditions which she handed to the Army on their arrival in Derry prior to dismantling the barricades. One of the conditions was a general amnesty for all those people defending their homes in the barricaded area. The barricades came down. However the Army Council and Blakemore's superiors still regarded my wife as a rioter. (*Pause.*) There is one thing you should know. Eighteen months ago at Sandhurst, I did try to meet Kitson. I asked Blakemore to arrange a meeting for me. I had very selfish reasons for doing so. I wanted to interview him for a paper I was giving at a conference in Stockholm on Insecurity and the State. It would have been a great coup. When I suggested a drink with Kitson either at the mess or at the house, Blakemore refused point blank. My brother-in-law doesn't like him – Kitson has no small talk. My family has nothing but. (*Pause.*) When Rosa left me, she said she regarded all her association with me as a betrayal of her tribe. I really didn't know what she meant at the time. I was deeply mortified and ashamed. Because I do believe she was happy with me once.

(*A long pause. Then* JOSIE *comes back to the table.*)

JOSIE: Joe.

(JOE *looks up.*)

It's finished.

(*She picks up the file and puts it back in her bag. She holds out her hand to him.*)

Welcome. To the tribe.

(JOE *gets to his feet half dazed. She walks quickly away, followed by* JOE. *A door bangs. They have gone, the room is in darkness. Someone strikes a match, and we are alerted to the presence of two men.* MALACHY *lights a cigarette for* CATHAL O'DONNELL.)

MALACHY: Well, Cathal, I think we have a new man.

O'DONNELL: I must stop this. (*Holding the lighted cigarette out for inspection*) Filthy habit. The wife – doesn't approve.

ACT TWO

SCENE I

DONNA, LIAM, JOSIE.

DONNA *is sitting on a straight-backed chair, alone in the living room. There is a light on her face, the rest is darkness.*

DONNA: The devil's back. He was lying with his head on my pillow this morning. When I woke up I recognized him immediately. Even though it's been years. (*Pause.*) The first time I ever saw him, he was standing in the corner of the room. I could feel something watching me. I had the bedclothes tucked up almost to my nose, so that I had to peer carefully round the room – and there he was. He seemed to grow out of the corner until he was towering over me. I panicked because I felt I was suffocating. My first husband was with me at the time. He called a doctor. He said I had asthma. The funny thing was, I really didn't get over my asthma attacks until my husband was interned. And I haven't seen the devil since. (*Pause.*) Until this morning. Liam bent over and kissed me goodbye as he was leaving. The trouble was he blocked my mouth and I couldn't breathe through my nose so I kept having to break away from him. When he'd gone, I closed my eyes and tried to get some sleep before the child woke. That was when I heard the door open. I thought Liam had come back so I opened my eyes, and there he was, the devil. If he had any hair at all it was red. He climbed on top of the bed and put his head on the pillow next to me. I felt so sick at the sight of him because I knew I didn't have the strength to struggle any more. I said: 'Please leave me alone.' I was very surprised when he replied. He's never spoken to me before. He said very quietly, 'All right, Donna.' And do you know – he vanished. But I don't believe he's really gone. He never really goes away.

(*She begins to have an attack. She starts to vomit or choke twice, but nothing happens. Recovers. The door opens into the room, throwing light across the floor. A figure stands in the light of the doorway.*)

Who is it?

LIAM: Who were you expecting?

(*He switches on the light and closes the door. Almost tripping over luggage he crosses the room.*)

What's this? Are you leaving me?

DONNA: I told you – Josie's moving back home.

LIAM: What's the matter with you?

DONNA: I'm tired.

LIAM: You're tired all the time now. I think maybe you're tired of me.

DONNA: Liam, what are you saying?

LIAM: It's been three weeks since I came out of the Kesh, and all I hear is that you're tired.

DONNA: Catherine kept me awake all night. I'm exhausted.

LIAM: You were never exhausted with your husband!

(DONNA *rushes around the room closing the doors.*)

DONNA: Please don't fight with me in front of Josie.

LIAM: (*Raising his voice*) I'm not fighting with you.

DONNA: Please don't shout. She'll hear you. I'll feel so humiliated.

LIAM: But it's true. It's him you want.

DONNA: Please, Liam. Please lower your voice. She'll think you don't love me and then it'll be difficult for me to feel good about myself and I'll have to leave here for shame and I've nowhere else to go.

LIAM: Go on, say it. I revolt you. You can't stand the sight of me.

DONNA: Oh Jesus God, I wish I were dead.

LIAM: It's true, admit it. Admit it. It's him, isn't it?

DONNA: No. No. I've loved only you. I always loved only you.

LIAM: But you married him!

DONNA: You've got to stop tormenting me because I had a husband. I was a girl then!

LIAM: Why don't you love me Donna?

DONNA: I cried all the way up the aisle. I told you that before. I was pregnant, they made me marry him. He was fifteen years older than me. I told him, I didn't love him. He said, 'Try to love me, then one day you will.' But I couldn't, because I'd always loved you. Oh, I did ever since I was a child.
(LIAM *is utterly immobile and unmoved during her entreaty.*)
Oh Liam, remember I used to come and have my bath with Josie and Frieda on Friday nights. And you used to pretend not to notice us. And then one Friday night you came into the parlour and said, 'What's happening?' And we said we were having a party and we were putting our money together for lemonade and crisps and you said, 'Well, here's some silver towards your party.' And Josie said you'd never given them a penny before towards anything. It was because I was there. And I blushed and laughed. Oh, I've loved you since I was nine years old.
(*For the first time he turns to her.*)

LIAM: But you married him!

DONNA: Oh Liam. Liam! You know why.

LIAM: You had him first.

DONNA: You went away! You went away that summer!

LIAM: I had work to do.

DONNA: But you went away, you went to the Republic.

LIAM: I was wanted. We feared internment.

DONNA: And when you came back you had a girlfriend from Dublin. God, you had so many. I started going with Peter McNamee after that because I was lonely and he was kind to me. I left him for you. I gave up my son for you. As soon as you wanted me, I came. What more can I do?

LIAM: It wasn't just McNamee. There were others. They told me. They'd all had you. After the dances.

DONNA: Oh Jesus God!

LIAM: In the Kesh they told me about you after the dances. They all had you. But now you don't want me! Were they better than me, was that it?
(DONNA *takes up a knife from the table, and hands it to him.*)

DONNA: Take it. Kill me, love. Kill me. Kill me.

LIAM: No!

DONNA: Kill me. You want to kill me. Please.

LIAM: No! (*He throws the knife away.*)

DONNA: I can't do any more. I love you. I have always loved you. I gave away my only son for you. Because he looked like Peter. If you don't believe that I love you – I wish I were dead. I wish I were dead.

LIAM: Don't say that, Donna.

DONNA: I wish I were dead.

LIAM: I just had to find out.

(LIAM *ruffles her hair.*)

I love you so much you see. And I can't get enough of you. When I'm away, things prey on my mind. I kept remembering all those years before we went out together and all the other men in your life. And I thought because I'm not around so much you'd find someone else.

DONNA: I won't find anyone else. I promise. You mean everything to me.

LIAM: I'd like to go to bed now.

DONNA: I can't! Josie's upstairs.

LIAM: (*Becoming cold again*) All right. I'll be back in an hour.

DONNA: Liam! Please. Where are you going?

LIAM: I'm going to the club!

(*He leaves, slamming the door.* DONNA *sinks down, beginning to cry; only* JOSIE*'s rapid footsteps on the stair force her to pull herself together.*)

JOSIE: (*Bursts open the door from the stairway carrying an armful of dresses on hangers.*) Was that our Liam? (DONNA *nods.* JOSIE *leaves the dresses over the cases.*) I was hoping for a lift. He uses this place like a cloakroom. (*Coming back to* DONNA) My daddy'll be along later to pick this stuff up.

DONNA: I wish you weren't going.

JOSIE: So do I. I'm dreading it. He treats me like a kid!

DONNA: Why don't you stay?

JOSIE: Three's a crowd. Anyway, I think you and Liam need time together. You should have a wee holiday.

DONNA: Yes, I know. He said he would take us away somewhere hot. Where are you off to now?

JOSIE: Dublin for the weekend – with Joe Conran.

DONNA: Do you see much of him?

JOSIE: We're working together. (*Hurrying*) Bye-bye.
(*She kisses* DONNA.)

DONNA: Nice perfume. Lemons?

JOSIE: Joe gave it to me. He got it duty free on his last trip to Amsterdam.

DONNA: What are you getting so defensive about? I just said you smelt of lemons.

JOSIE: (*At the door*) What'll I bring you back from Dublin?

DONNA: (*Waving her away*) Yourself.

JOSIE: I'll see you.
(JOSIE *smiles and leaves the room.* DONNA *is smiling as well.*)

SCENE 2

MCDERMOT, FRIEDA.

A room in JOHN MCDERMOT'*s house. He is on the telephone. The clasped hands symbol of the Party is on the wall, along with the slogan:* 'Democracy against Direct Rule'. *The room reflects that his political commitment is not separate from his domestic arrangements. The telephone cradle stands on a chair.*

MCDERMOT: Well, obviously it's very dangerous, it will set back the cause of Irish unity another – (*Pause.*) You're not interested in Irish unity? Thank you.
(FRIEDA *arrives with a handful of leaflets. She has been outside.* MCDERMOT *puts down the phone.*)
That's the third trade unionist out of seven who refuses to discuss the Petition against the Amendment. It's unbelievable. They've all said the same thing – no interest in the politics of the Republic.

FRIEDA: What's the Petition against the Amendment?

MCDERMOT: (*Going towards her*) Do you mean to tell me that you haven't even read the leaflets you're handing out?

FRIEDA: I was rushing.

MCDERMOT: That's no excuse.

FRIEDA: Och, what is it about? It'll save me reading it. I hate political pamphlets. Anyway, you always explain things better than you write them.

MCDERMOT: I don't think there's anybody who has insulted me more than you have – in my life.

FRIEDA: You're awful easy insulted. I'm the same with everybody.

MCDERMOT: (*Sighs.*) There's to be a referendum in the Republic to decide whether the Constitution should be amended to include an anti-abortion clause. Abortion is already illegal in the South; by putting it into the Constitution it cannot be challenged or even changed. Do you see? It's the Catholic Church barricading itself into the Constitution.

FRIEDA: (*Putting the leaflet down*) I wouldn't sign that petition.

MCDERMOT: You don't agree with abortion as a civil right for Protestants in the South?

FRIEDA: I don't really regard the politics of Southern Ireland as having anything to do with me.

MCDERMOT: Well, that is truly extraordinary.

FRIEDA: It's a foreign country as far as I'm concerned.

MCDERMOT: I think you're taking your rebellion against your father a bit far. Surely you want a united Ireland by democratic consent?

FRIEDA: No, it's not even that, I just don't care if Ireland is united or not.

MCDERMOT: What do you care about?

FRIEDA: I just want to sing my own songs.

MCDERMOT: (*Ironic*) Is that all?

FRIEDA: (*Misunderstanding*) It's everything. When the lights go down and I'm standing in a spotlight. There's a tremor; it starts in my toes and roots me to the floor when the first note comes. I'm pulled away to somewhere else entirely. There's nothing like it. Except that I want to do it again and again.

MCDERMOT: I used to feel like that a long time ago when I made political speeches. But I don't any more. Maybe it's the size of the audience these days. (*Pause.*) Have you ever cared about a person the way you care about singing?

FRIEDA: I don't believe in love, if that's what you mean.

MCDERMOT: What about caring for a friend? A person? (FRIEDA *shakes her head.*) You see, I'm in politics because I care for people. But I care most of all for one person, and have for some time. Frieda, I care about you.

FRIEDA: Don't say that! I'll only disappoint you. (*He takes advantage of her confusion and kisses her. She responds momentarily, and then breaks away.*) Oh I hate you!

MCDERMOT: No, you don't.

FRIEDA: I do. You've gone and spoiled everything.

MCDERMOT: You wanted me to spoil it. You were furious when my girlfriend came out of the bathroom the other morning.

FRIEDA: That was because she was having a bath when I wanted a pee.

MCDERMOT: And you were very annoyed when I stayed away last night. All night.

FRIEDA: Ha! The vanity of it!

MCDERMOT: You sulked all through breakfast. In fact you manage to sulk every time I bring a woman into the house. I can't persuade anyone to spend the night any more because your hostility makes them so uncomfortable.

FRIEDA: If that's what you think, there is a solution.

MCDERMOT: I think so, too.

FRIEDA: I'd better move out.

MCDERMOT: Alternatively I could kiss you again, and we could go to bed this afternoon.

FRIEDA: You're smiling.

MCDERMOT: I've been smiling from the beginning. And I've wanted you for a long time. Why do you think I invited you to stay with me?

(*He attempts to kiss her again, but she moves away immediately.*)

FRIEDA: I can't. You're my friend. You're the only friend I've got now. If I sleep with you, you won't be my friend any more. And I'll have to find somewhere else to live. And frankly, I don't feel like it.

MCDERMOT: What are you afraid of?

FRIEDA: I'm not afraid. (*Furious*) I've never run away from anything in my life.

MCDERMOT: You've never run away from a fight. But there are other areas of experience. (*Makes another attempt to touch her.*) Frieda, (*very kindly*) I'm very good in bed.

FRIEDA: (*Enraged. Hits him in the chest.*) I hate you, John McDermot.

(*She throws the pamphlets across the room and exits.*)

MCDERMOT: Frieda! What did I say?

(*The phone rings.* MCDERMOT *is not sure whether to pick it up.*)

Frieda! Please come back!

(*The phone rings until he picks it up.*)

Hello? . . . Yes, this is John McDermot . . . yes, I did call you earlier . . . It's about the Petition against the Amendment. I'm collecting signatures from prominent trade unionists and people like yourself. It's for an open letter we want to publish in the 'Irish Times' . . . (FRIEDA *arrives with a suitcase. He begins to signal to her while talking on the phone, but she refuses to respond.*)

What's that? . . . Look, can I ring you back? . . . You've caught me at a difficult moment . . . Yes, of course . . . Goodbye. (*Puts the phone down.*)

FRIEDA: Can I use that phone please? I want to ring for a taxi.

MCDERMOT: What are you doing? (*She sits down on her suitcase.*) I thought you didn't want to be homeless.

FRIEDA: I find your confidence both in relation to me, other women, and the rest of the world nothing short of nauseous. You behave as if you had nothing to learn, nothing to discover, no problems, and everybody else was waiting for you to fuck them!

MCDERMOT: I'm sure you're right.

FRIEDA: But what I really hate is the idea of having to trade something for my being here.

MCDERMOT: My intention wasn't to trade. I wanted you. And I didn't repress it. That's all. The house is yours; there's no price.

(*She proceeds to pick up the phone book. He seems about to leave the room and give up, when he stops.*)

Where will you go?

FRIEDA: As far away from you as possible. I'll resign from the Party.

MCDERMOT: And what reason will you give for that?

FRIEDA: Personal reasons.

MCDERMOT: There are no personal reasons any more. Everything is political.

FRIEDA: I've heard that before!

MCDERMOT: When you joined the Party you promised to secure working class unity – Catholic and Protestant – before the real struggle could begin. I can't see that my personal behaviour towards you should make any difference to your commitment to that idea.

FRIEDA: On the contrary, I tend to judge ideas by the people who utter them.

MCDERMOT: (*Sighs.*) That's just the trouble, Frieda. Your standards are so high.

(*She is arrested by the remark for a moment. Then she closes the telephone book, puts it down and reaches for the phone. Beginning to dial the number.*)

Frieda. (*He stops her.*) Listen to me. I'll miss you. I'll miss you messing up the house. I'll miss you leaving all the dishes for me to wash. Leaving all the lights on. Running up the heating bills. I'll miss you letting the fire go out, and then not being able to relight it. I'll miss your awful singing in the bath. Being rude to my friends, particularly when they're women. Most of all I'll miss the way you change your mind. You're so much trouble, Frieda, would you do one thing – one thing I wouldn't miss?

FRIEDA: What?

MCDERMOT: Would you stay?

FRIEDA: (*Overcome. Moving towards him*) Do I really annoy you that much?

MCDERMOT: Yes.

FRIEDA: Am I really that much trouble?

MCDERMOT: Yes.

(*They kiss, for a long time.*)

SCENE 3

JOSIE, JOE.

Dublin. A hotel bedroom. JOSIE *is sitting up on the bed staring at an eighteenth-century doorway.* JOE *is lying back, listening sleepily.*

JOSIE: It's strange you bringing me here.

JOE: Why?

JOSIE: That time I told you about, when I first came to Dublin, I walked round for hours just looking at the place. I passed this hotel but I didn't notice it. I had my head down against the rain until a glass coach drew up alongside me.

JOE: And a beautiful girl got out wearing glass slippers!

JOSIE: There was a bride and groom in it. They were coming in here. There were some people in gold braid on the steps, they were standing on red carpet, through the window you could see the chandeliers, and above it all a tricolour was flying . . . It was the same flag that one July my father flew from our upstairs window. I'd have braved a baton charge to get that flag back from the police who snatched it. And I did . . . Yet nothing in the world would have induced me to defy the grandness of this place. I felt as if they'd snatched the flag away again . . . That's why it's so strange you bringing me here.

JOE: I can't imagine you lacking in courage, Josie.

JOSIE: Oh, I frequently do . . . Have you ever killed anyone?

(*He begins to sit up.*)

JOE: I can't say that I have.

JOSIE: Not even as a soldier?

JOE: I trained as an engineer.

JOSIE: Oh yes.

JOE: Have you ever killed anyone?

JOSIE: I planted a bomb once. It didn't go off.

JOE: Why?

JOSIE: I don't know, some technical fault.

JOE: No, I mean why did you plant a bomb?

JOSIE: I was fed up being a courier . . . They used women as messengers then. I wanted to show them I could take the same risks as a man. So I planned it, stole the car, and left it outside the law courts. I'm glad it didn't go off.

JOE: You did this entirely on your own?

JOSIE: No. A man I'd have gone to hell for helped me.

JOE: When was this?

JOSIE: In the early seventies. We were all a little bit mad then. Me especially.

JOE: So you wouldn't do it again?

JOSIE: I've lost the killing instinct. Now, I tend to think the crushing of a foetus is a tragedy.

JOE: Well, that's up to you.

JOSIE: Have you ever loved anyone so much you would die for them?

JOE: This is fun, Josie. I want what there is between us to begin and end in this room. And then on another occasion we could go to another room and have some more fun.

JOSIE: Fun! I hate that word.

(*He reaches out to stroke her hair.*)

JOE: I'm sorry if I offended you.

(*He kisses her.*)

Do you know him well?

JOSIE: Who?

JOE: O'Donnell.

JOSIE: He taught me how to build a barricade. (*She looks at her watch.*) And he doesn't like to be kept waiting.

(JOE *gets out of bed, goes to the bathroom en suite, leaving the door open. Immediate sound of ablutions.* JOSIE *finds herself entirely alone. The sound of ablutions gradually fades as she*

begins to speak.)
(*Speaking aloud*) Bus stop posts; manhole covers; telephone kiosk doors; traffic signs; corrugated iron fencing; and old doors, wood is best not glass; especially if you don't have an upturned bus or lorry. And a tape measure is useful too, to measure the mouth of the street . . . He held one end of the tape and I had the other. It was the first time I'd ever seen him. He kept shouting at me to hold still. Hurry up. Move quickly. Find the rope, nails, wood. He was so precise. And I kept coming back with what he wanted every time . . . All day we ran about measuring, hammering, securing, until towards evening we needed only two slim posts and it was finished. I remember we rushed off to the park to uproot some young trees, saplings the Corporation planted. We were high up on the bank when a woman passed. She was pushing a pram; a pregnant woman in a headscarf, then she waved. It was my first whole day with him. 'It's my wife,' he said. Safe. I'm safe from him. The sight of her large and alone, thoughts in her child on the womb and in the pram were battleship enough to keep me away. Until minutes later I slipped, slid down the wet bank after him and came to a halt. 'I can't get down,' I said. And he reached out his hand . . . I wasn't safe. I was lost.
(JOE *returns, dressed. He watches from the doorway.*)

SCENE 4

FRIEDA, MCDERMOT, FIRST POLICEMAN, SECOND POLICEMAN.
Two swings. A litter bin. Sounds of a children's playground.
FRIEDA *comes on.*

FRIEDA: This is a good place. (*Looking skyward*)
(MCDERMOT *comes on, also looking skyward.*)
There'll be hundreds here. (*Running with her hands outstretched*)

This one's mine. (*Pause.*) How many have you got?

MCDERMOT: I wasn't counting.

FRIEDA: You've got to count them. That's the whole point.

MCDERMOT: I'm not very good at this. It's not easy.

FRIEDA: Listen . . .

MCDERMOT: It's too calm.

(*She looks round. He takes a notebook out of his pocket to write in.*)

FRIEDA: Ah you're not going to do that again.

(*He walks away to the swing and sits down.*)

MCDERMOT: There's not enough wind.

FRIEDA: It won't be long.

(*She follows him and sits down on the second swing.*)

What is it anyway?

MCDERMOT: A piece for the paper on the by-election in Area H.

FRIEDA: Where's Area H?

MCDERMOT: North Belfast.

FRIEDA: Why can't they call it that? Why do you have to be a computer these days before you get any information? (*Pause. Waiting*) How did we do?

MCDERMOT: Four hundred and seventy-four votes out of a total poll of 6,881. Seven per cent of the poll. Not bad. We seem to be a growing force in the north of the city.

FRIEDA: John . . . there was a man following me in the rose gardens. I wasn't taking much notice – and then everywhere I turned he seemed to follow. When I stopped, he stopped. He was blocking the only way out. I had to run through the rose beds to get away from him.

MCDERMOT: Where was I when this was happening?

FRIEDA: I think you were in the Tropical Ravine. My arms are all scratched!

MCDERMOT: I suppose you thought he wanted to assault you? Not everybody does you know.

FRIEDA: He wasn't looking at me like that. He frightened me! His eyes were like ice. It felt as if he were deliberately marking me.

MCDERMOT: Why would he do that?

FRIEDA: Intimidation!

MCDERMOT: Your head's cut! This is a university district. It's always been safe.

FRIEDA: For some people nowhere is safe. (*Suddenly looks up.*) Oh look! We're missing our chance. (*She gets up from the swing and runs forward, looking skyward, her arms outstretched, hands cupped.*) I've got one. (*She runs first to the left a little, then to the right, as if chasing something. Claps her hands suddenly.*) Missed!

(MCDERMOT *starts up.*)

MCDERMOT: I see one.

(*He runs forward, towards it, and then follows it off. Voice off. Claps hands.*) Got it!

FRIEDA: Oh, I see another. (*She follows it as before, running about. She claps her hands together.*) Missed it! Damn!

(*A Land Rover screeches to a halt. Door slams. A* POLICEMAN *in a bullet-proof jacket approaches* FRIEDA, *who is standing with her eyes trained skyward.*)

FIRST POLICEMAN: What's going on here?

(FRIEDA *starts to rush off.*)

FRIEDA: There's another gust of wind –

(*The* POLICEMAN *grabs her arm.*)

FIRST POLICEMAN: I'm speaking to you.

FRIEDA: (*Indignant*) Shit! I've lost it.

(MCDERMOT *appears, holding his head.*)

MCDERMOT: I nearly knocked myself out that time.

(*A* SECOND POLICEMAN *in a bullet-proof jacket approaches. He too is looking skyward. Everyone is looking skyward.*)

SECOND POLICEMAN: Is there something up there?

(*Everyone looks at* FRIEDA.)

FRIEDA: Yes. Leaves.

FIRST POLICEMAN: Leaves?

FRIEDA: Yeah. It's autumn and the leaves are falling. So what you have to do is stand under a really big tree and wait till they fall.

SECOND POLICEMAN: Why?

FRIEDA: You have to try and catch them before they reach the ground. And for every one you catch you have one happy day next year. So I was standing here trying to catch three hundred and sixty-five, before you came along.
(*She looks skyward again.*)

FIRST POLICEMAN: Are you trying to make a fool of us?

MCDERMOT: No. Look. We're terribly sorry. She was a bit depressed, so we thought we'd come out and catch a few leaves to cheer her up!

FIRST POLICEMAN: You realize you're causing an obstruction.

FRIEDA: (*Looking up*) That's the intention.

FIRST POLICEMAN: We've had a number of complaints from the residents here that you two people have been causing a disturbance.

SECOND POLICEMAN: Do you live around here?

MCDERMOT: We live close by. We didn't realize we'd upset anyone. We'll go home now. Come on, Frieda.
(*He begins to take her away. She stops.*)

FRIEDA: Wait a minute. Do they not know about catching leaves, the people who complained about us?

SECOND POLICEMAN: Go on home now. Before you cause any more trouble.

MCDERMOT: Come on, Frieda.

FRIEDA: Trouble? Is it trouble to want to be happy? Do you not know about catching leaves? Do you not remember?
(MCDERMOT *and* FRIEDA *go. The* FIRST POLICEMAN *goes off in the opposite direction. The* SECOND POLICEMAN *looks up skyward for a moment. Sound of a Land Rover engine starting. He too hurries off. A leaf flutters down.*)

SCENE 5

DONNA, JOSIE, FIRST SOLDIER, SECOND SOLDIER, POLICEMAN.

Donna's living room. There is a glass of red wine on a low table and a bottle of pills. A small child's toy, a musical ball, is on the floor. DONNA *comes into the room followed by* JOSIE.

JOSIE: Liam said you were upset.

DONNA: Upset? Catherine fell down the stairs. Her head must have hit every step on the way down. Liam was right behind her. He couldn't stop it.

JOSIE: Is she all right?

DONNA: I sometimes think men don't actually like children – she's all right. She's made of rubber. I feel sick every time I think of it.

JOSIE: What are the pills for?

DONNA: The doctor gave me them – to calm me down.

JOSIE: Donna, I've something to tell you.

DONNA: Has he left his wife for you yet?

JOSIE: She left him ages ago.

DONNA: She's a braver woman than I thought. She's eight months pregnant.

JOSIE: Where did you hear that?

DONNA: Everybody knows Mairead O'Donnell's pregnant.

JOSIE: Not Cathal! I was talking about Joe.

DONNA: I can't keep up with this! Three months ago you had my head turned – you were so passionately in love with Cathal O'Donnell.

JOSIE: I know, but . . . have you ever thought, is this the man who has come to love me?

DONNA: You're not wise.

JOSIE: Oh Donna. I owe him so much. I'm really beginning to feel healed. I even forgot about Cathal. He took all the pain away!

(CATHERINE *begins to cry.* DONNA *goes to the door and listens. It stops. Then crying continues.*)

DONNA: I'm in for a bad night.

(*She exits.* JOSIE *listens also.*)

(*Voice off*) All right, lamb pie. Mammy's coming!

(JOSIE, *very thoughtful, picks up the musical ball. It tinkles gently when lifted, and again as she moves it at her ear.*)

JOSIE: Fuck! (*Drops it.*) Donna! It's the Brits.

(DONNA *runs back into the room.*)

DONNA: Get out! Leave me!

JOSIE: Can you cope?

DONNA: Leave me! They can't take me away if there's nobody to look after the child.

(JOSIE *exits quickly through the front door, which she doesn't have time to close. The sound of Landrovers screeching to a halt and doors slamming, followed by heavily shod feet running.* DONNA *takes up the bottle of pills in time to face the first of two armed soldiers who come through the open door.*)

Where are the RUC? You're not allowed to raid our houses without a member of the police being present.

FIRST SOLDIER: Don't get smart.

(*A* POLICEMAN *enters, and waits quietly in the background. The* SECOND SOLDIER *begins to look around.*)

Where is he?

(DONNA *watches the* SOLDIER *who has gone out to search the rooms.*)

DONNA: Don't waken the child. Where's who?

FIRST SOLDIER: Your husband.

DONNA: My husband's in the Crumlin Road Gaol. I haven't seen him for ten years.

POLICEMAN: We're looking for Liam McCoy.

DONNA: I don't know. I haven't seen him.

POLICEMAN: He lives here.

DONNA: Only when it suits him.

FIRST SOLDIER: So where is he?

DONNA: I don't know. You know what it's like. He goes out, gets drunk and forgets to come back. It's not against the law you know.

(*The* SECOND SOLDIER *comes back. He is carrying two small firearms in a towel. He presents it to her.*)

You planted it.

SECOND SOLDIER: (*To the* FIRST SOLDIER) Loose floorboard at the top of the stairs.

FIRST SOLDIER: You could do three years for this.

DONNA: How could I do three years? You won't find my prints on them.

FIRST SOLDIER: (*To the* POLICEMAN) What about that other

address? (*The* POLICEMAN *hands him a piece of paper.*) Two-six-two Grosvenor Road. (*They wait for* DONNA*'s reaction.*) Maybe she knows where he is.

SECOND SOLDIER: Must be with Eileen tonight.

FIRST SOLDIER: Have you met Eileen? Dark hair. Slim. Very nice. Sure you don't know her?

(*Bin lids start up.*)

DONNA: Get out! Get out of my house!

(CATHERINE *begins to cry loudly.*)

SECOND SOLDIER: I'm sure Eileen knows where he is?

DONNA: If you don't leave me alone I'll take these pills. I mean it. I'll swallow the lot!

(*She puts the bottle to her mouth and begins to swallow the pills. Some fall on the floor, scattering.*)

POLICEMAN: (*Coming forward*) Hey, hey.

(*The* SOLDIERS *withdraw quickly.*)

Now, now. Nobody's going to harm you. It's your man they're after.

(*The bin lids die down with the* SOLDIERS' *exit.* DONNA *stops, looks round at the policeman.* CATHERINE *cries out again.*)

What age is the baby?

DONNA: Fuck off!

(*The* POLICEMAN *exits.* DONNA *sits down and pours the rest of the pills into her hand; she looks at the glass of wine. Catherine's crying reaches a pitch of screaming. The bin lids get louder. Darkness. Every sound stops.*)

SCENE 6

JOSIE, O'DONNELL, LIAM, MALACHY, DANNY, DONNA.

The Club. A room off the main bar. CATHAL O'DONNELL *is sitting at a small café table. The scene is similar to the room arrangement when* JOSIE *interrogated* JOE CONRAN. *There is an empty chair opposite* CATHAL; *he seems to be waiting.* JOSIE *comes in. She has not expected to find herself alone with* O'DONNELL.

JOSIE: I was told my brother was here.

O'DONNELL: He's all right.

JOSIE: Donna's house was raided.

O'DONNELL: Yes, we heard.

JOSIE: I think someone should go and see if she's all right. I wasn't able to go back. (*Pause.*) I suppose he realizes that he can't go home. (*She turns to go.*)

O'DONNELL: Josie!

JOSIE: I've got to find Joe – I don't want him walking into a patrol.

O'DONNELL: He's gone home. I want to talk to you.

JOSIE: So I hear.

O'DONNELL: Did Joe tell you about his assignment?

JOSIE: No. Of course not!

O'DONNELL: That's very professional of him.

JOSIE: He is – I cleared him, remember.

O'DONNELL: Oh yes . . . So you think it's an impossibility? (*She looks confused.*) The thirty-two-county workers' republic. A place we will never come into.

JOSIE: You were there!

O'DONNELL: You never said that to me.

JOSIE: You don't trust anyone. Do you Cathal?

O'DONNELL: You do yourself an injustice. I wanted to see him. I thought if I could see him – I would know.

JOSIE: And do you?

O'DONNELL: Yes. It's really very simple. He's a romantic. Sit down. (*Pause.* JOSIE *sits reluctantly.* O'DONNELL *immediately gets to his feet.*) I've put Conran in charge of arms purchasing. The whole operation. And stockpiling for the period after British Withdrawal. That's why I wanted to talk to you. He's going to meet the Libyans in Malta next month. The idea is that he will do the buying abroad but I'd like you to find the locations in Ireland where the stuff can be kept until it's needed. (*Pause.*) Well, are you happy about that? Do you see any problems?

JOSIE: Since when has my happiness been a priority of yours?

O'DONNELL: Oh I see. You're going to be vengeful.

JOSIE: I'm not going to be vengeful. My wounds are healed. But I am just a little surprised and suspicious that I am being consulted about something I am usually told to do. (O'DONNELL *sits down again opposite her*.)

O'DONNELL: Are we talking about this assignment or are we talking about something else? If we're talking about your assignments, you have always been consulted by me. I have always taken your advice. I have always trusted your instincts and your judgement. If we're talking about something else, then I suggest that you say so. But don't infect your political judgement with emotional considerations!

JOSIE: You were never very keen to separate them before.

O'DONNELL: I did try to talk to you in Dublin, but you ran away from me.

JOSIE: You know damn well what I'm complaining about. Your interest in me was to do with your desires, your appetites, your needs, which were fortunately once coincidental with mine. Now they're clearly not!

O'DONNELL: Once? Once coincidental?

JOSIE: Yes. They ceased to coincide when you let go of me five months ago!

O'DONNELL: Not for me.

JOSIE: Oh please. You cut me off! You sat at meetings ignoring me. You made sure that you and I were never alone. I got my orders through other people all of a sudden. You put the whole power of this organization between us, so I could never get a chance to ask you why. For ten years you have been my only lover, and because it was never publicly acknowledged no one ever understood my grief. (*Pause*.) You came out of that meeting in Dublin and you said, 'Are you around?' What did you expect me to say? 'Yes.' For your pleasure?

O'DONNELL: Five months ago I had to leave you and return to my wife. She was pregnant again. As you know, her last pregnancy miscarried. She has no family, unlike you. She has no one to turn to but me. She depends on me totally.

And she's tenaciously loyal. Because I was sent word that she'd been so ill, and because of being married to me, she was having a very difficult time – the house was raided twice in a month – I came north to take her back across the border. It was not easy for me to stop seeing you, but there was nothing else for it. Since Mairead and I have been living together again I rediscovered what I'd forgotten – that my wife is not the passion in my life, you are. I once told you that I'd never let you down.

JOSIE: You said you'd never let her down either.

O'DONNELL: I intend to keep my promise. I don't intend to choose between you.

JOSIE: I'm afraid you'll have to.

O'DONNELL: I can't live without you. I have tried. I fought the memory of you every day. But you are the one who is with me in my thoughts all the time, not her; it's your voice I want to hear when she speaks, not hers.

JOSIE: I've begun again with someone else.

O'DONNELL: I can't let you go. It's not over.

JOSIE: (*Almost laughing*) Oh, it's not over. For months there was no one. Until Joe Conran appears. Then suddenly you notice, and it's not over! Well, it is for me.

O'DONNELL: I understand why you're with him. But you also need me. I see no reason why our friendship shouldn't continue. I don't let go of my friends easily.

(JOSIE *gets up from the table.*)

JOSIE: I hope that's not a threat!

O'DONNELL: It's not a threat. How could I threaten you when the whole apparatus of the British State doesn't cause you a hair's turn! Josie, I still love you.

JOSIE: Love? You once told me that to love something was to confer a greater existence on it – you were talking about patriotism – the love of your country. I've only recently realized that you never loved me. You took me. You possessed me. You took my youth and you hid it in a dark corner for a long time. You never draped me with a public celebration. But I'm out of the corner. It's over. The hiding is finished. You are in my thoughts from time to time, I admit; but usually as a prelude to a nightmare. (*Getting up*) If you've nothing else to say, I'd like to go. I've no wish to discuss 'other business' with you. You can send your messages through the usual channels.

O'DONNELL: All right, Josie. But it's not over yet!

JOSIE: (*Turning*) Six months ago I'd have died for you. Five weeks ago, even, I might have listened. Now – it's too late.

O'DONNELL: Why is it too late? What has so many weeks got to do with it?

JOSIE: I'm going to have his child.

(*He is visibly devastated.*)

(*Relentless*) I'm pregnant too.

(*He attempts a recovery.*)

O'DONNELL: Congratulations.

JOSIE: Thanks.

(*She walks away to the exit door. Turns again.*)

Goodbye Cathal.

(*She exits. He is left alone sitting at the table. He smiles through his teeth, takes a packet of cigarettes from his pocket, stops smiling, crushes the cigarette packet, goes off, passing* MALACHY *and* LIAM *on his way out.*)

LIAM: Was that Cathal?

MALACHY: Aye.

LIAM: What's he looking so pleased about?

MALACHY: He's not. He's got an ulcer; he always smiles when it hurts. (*He puts his empty glass down.*) Will you take another wee drink? (LIAM *shakes his head.*) What's wrong with you tonight?

LIAM: I'm worried about Josie. I don't know how you could let her do it.

MALACHY: What else could I do? She said: 'I want to go and live with him.' I said: 'Over my dead body.' She said: 'I'm having his baby.' I said: 'Fair enough. I'll help you move.' What was I supposed to do? I'm no good with wee babies.

(*The* TWO MEN *move down the table with their pint glasses and set them down.*)

LIAM: She hardly knows him.

MALACHY: Well, she'll get to know him better now!

LIAM: You should never have let her move out of the house in the first place.

MALACHY: Don't you lay that at my door. It was your idea that she moved in with Donna. If you hadn't been so paranoid about your wife running off with somebody while you were in the Kesh, Josie would still be at home with me now.
(DONNA *comes in like a ghost, unseen, and waits.*)
At least he's on our side. Not like that other wee bitch running off with a Stickie!

LIAM: We hope he's on our side.

MALACHY: Ah now, don't you start that again. He's off to Malta with four and a half million of our money; you can be sure we checked him out.

LIAM: I just don't trust Conran. It's funny my house being raided.

DONNA: Your house?
(*Both men turn.*)

LIAM: Donna!

MALACHY: Would you take a wee drink? (*Senses danger.*) Gabriel's got three tons of sugar.
(MALACHY *senses danger and exits quickly.*)

LIAM: (*Pause.*) I'm sorry about what happened.
(*She walks up to him and hits him with her fist on the side of the head. The blow stuns him. He reels momentarily. He never takes his eyes off her.*)
All right Donna. (*Backing off*) All right.
(*He backs away and then turns and hurries off to another part of the club. She turns and walks away towards the door out. She stops, puts her hand to her chest, breathing deeply. She appears to vomit or choke once, then twice. Nothing happens.* DANNY *appears quickly at her side. She is bent double and does not see who it is.*)

DANNY: Donna? Donna?
(*She straightens hopefully and discovers him.*)
Are you all right?

DONNA: Yes, I'm fine.
DANNY: What's wrong?
DONNA: Nothing. Please go away.
DANNY: You don't look very happy.
DONNA: Life's not a bed of roses.
DANNY: Can I walk you home? Please?
DONNA: If you like.
(*They exit.*)

SCENE 7

JOSIE, JOE.
Bedroom. JOE *is packing clothes into a bag.* JOSIE *comes into the room in her nightdress.*

JOE: What is it?
JOSIE: I'm bleeding again.
JOE: What can I do?
JOSIE: (*She gets into bed.*) I have to lie down and put my feet up. Can you put a pillow under my feet? (*He puts a pillow under her feet.*) I have to raise them higher than my head. (*She lies back.*) It happened a few days ago; but it stopped when I lay down. It's such a dangerous time . . . Oh God! I'd be so angry if I lost it.
JOE: You won't lose it, Josie. I know what that's like. My wife miscarried.
(*He lies down beside her.*)
JOSIE: If you'd had a child with your wife, would you have stayed with her?
JOE: If, if, if. Who can answer if?
JOSIE: What's wrong?
JOE: (*Pause.*) I was thinking about your brother.
JOSIE: Our Liam?
JOE: He's not happy.
JOSIE: Liam's never happy. He's stupid. He's on the run permanently.
(JOE *sits up.*)

JOE: I think he's resentful because I got the assignment he wanted.

JOSIE: That's right: foreign travel. He promised Donna a continental holiday when he got out of the Kesh.

JOE: I wish O'Donnell hadn't been so brutal with him. He said I spoke five modern languages, which is an absolute must for working abroad, while Liam only had Gaelic. The last thing I want is to make enemies here –

JOSIE: Joe! I want out!

JOE: Out? Out of what?

JOSIE: I'm tired. Tired of this endless night watch. I've been manning the barricades since 'sixty-nine. I'd like to stop for a while, look around me, plant a garden, listen for other sounds; the breathing of a child somewhere outside Andersonstown.

JOE: You constantly surprise me.

JOSIE: Do you know what I spent the last few days worrying about? An incident – the night Donna's house was raided. I was walking back from the club, there was a foot patrol in the street. I should have turned back immediately and warned the men. But I was so preoccupied I wasn't even aware of the Army until I walked right into them and nearly fell over a corporal sitting in a hawthorn hedge with his face blackened. He shouted something stupid after me like: 'This is a great place to come for a holiday.' And do you know what I was thinking about? Whether my womb would be big enough for the child. Because you're so big and I'm so small. I'm really worried that the baby might get too big too quickly and come out before it's finished.

JOE: You idiot!

JOSIE: I'm so afraid of losing it. It's like a beginning within me. For the first time the possibility of being happy. So I'm going to tell O'Donnell that I won't accept this or any other assignment.

JOE: Perhaps it's something you feel at the moment.

JOSIE: No. I don't want my mother's life!

JOE: Then why? Why are you having a child? You did this without asking me!

JOSIE: It was my decision – it had nothing to do with you.

JOE: It was our decision!

JOSIE: We grew up by the hearth and slept in cots at the fire. We escaped nothing and nothing escaped us . . . I wish I could go back.

JOE: Go back?

JOSIE: Yes, and remember . . . those first moments.

JOE: Remember what?

JOSIE: Back then . . . somehow rid myself of that dark figure which hovered about the edge of my cot – priest or police I can't tell – but the light is so dim in my memory – most of the room is in shadow – and gets dimmer all the time.

JOE: Josie!

JOSIE: I'm trying to tell you why – about the first few moments when I took the wrong way.

JOE: Josie! It's not what we saw through the bars of a cot or heard from the corner of a nursery that made us what we are.

JOSIE: You would say that.

JOE: It won't help you to remember, because it wasn't so individual.

JOSIE: The bleeding's stopped.

JOE: I came to this country because I tried to live the life you seem to want now. I tried it with someone else and it didn't work.

JOSIE: Rosa. That woman's name haunts me. Did she want children very much? And you didn't?

(*He gets off the bed quickly and paces the room.*)

JOE: I hate tots! Babies! I hate this whole fertility business! I'm not interested in fucking children!

JOSIE: (*Pause.*) I don't ask you for anything but to be with me until the birth.

JOE: Of course I'll be with you. But you mustn't depend on me, Rosa – (JOSIE *stares.* JOE *realizes.*) Josie.

(*He gets into bed beside her*) Let me hold you . . . Look, when I come back from Malta, I'll take you away for a while.

(*A long pause.*)

JOSIE: You don't have to worry about me, Joe. I've got two hearts.

SCENE 8

FRIEDA, MCDERMOT.

Bedroom in McDermot's flat in South Belfast.

A cacophony of cymbals, skin drums, tambourines from the street.

FRIEDA: What on earth's that?
(*She sits up in bed.*)
MCDERMOT: The Chinese restaurant are celebrating their sabbath.
FRIEDA: It's not very harmonious.
MCDERMOT: I think the year of the rat is about to begin.
(*She listens again.*)
FRIEDA: Stop it!
MCDERMOT: What?
FRIEDA: Don't be so innocent. You know what you are doing.
MCDERMOT: I was just exploring.
FRIEDA: John! . . . I've come seven times already, I can't come any more.
MCDERMOT: But I thought you liked it.
FRIEDA: I'm all confused. I have so many things to think about . . . what I'm going to do with my life . . . where I'm going to go next . . . I have plans to make but every time you make love to me my mind goes blank!
MCDERMOT: You're tired of me.
FRIEDA: Maybe I'm not just what you want, John . . . I want a wee bit of privacy.
MCDERMOT: Marry me?
(*Terrifying sound of breaking glass.*)
FRIEDA: God!
MCDERMOT: That wasn't a Chinese gong.
(*He leaps out of bed quickly and goes to the living room.* FRIEDA *follows him to the bedroom door, it looks immediately on to the hall.*)

FRIEDA: (*Calling out*) It's all your fault, John McDermot! I told you not to put up an election poster in the window.

MCDERMOT: (*Comes back. He is carrying a brick in one hand and a note in the other.*) Don't be such a harpy!

FRIEDA: You called me a harpy!

(*She snatches the note from him and reads. He sits down wearily on the bed and watches her.*)

I expected this. Now do you believe me?

MCDERMOT: About what?

FRIEDA: The man in the park.

MCDERMOT: Catch yourself on!

(*She moves across the bedroom to the hall.*)

FRIEDA: Time I was going.

MCDERMOT: Where to?

FRIEDA: Safety.

(*She drags a suitcase out of the hall.*)

MCDERMOT: I forgot, it's Sunday. You always run away on Sunday.

(*She is packing clothes into the case.*)

I thought you were banned from the ghetto.

FRIEDA: I'm not going back there. I was thinking of leaving the tribes behind. Both of them!

MCDERMOT: Are you talking about leaving the country again?

FRIEDA: Very definitely.

MCDERMOT: I ought to buy you a season ticket for the Liverpool boat. You pack that suitcase about three times a week. (*She continues packing.*) You'll be very unhappy. The Irish aren't popular where you're going. Thanks to your relatives.

FRIEDA: You think I'm popular here? (*She indicates the brick.*) Whatever England is – it's got to be better than this!

MCDERMOT: Oh, for heaven's sake! You're running away from a couple of drunks!

FRIEDA: A couple of drunks?

MCDERMOT: Yes. A couple of drunks who've had their moment of power over you. Why give in to them?

FRIEDA: I'm not so enamoured with my life here that it's something I could die defending.

MCDERMOT: Who said anything about dying?

FRIEDA: It said in that note that this is a Protestant street! I have no wish to contest that. You have every right to live here. I haven't.

MCDERMOT: Frieda! Nobody in this street knows anything about you. The brick was thrown by a couple of mindless yobbos.

FRIEDA: How do you know?

MCDERMOT: I teach those kids every day.

FRIEDA: Oh please don't try to dismiss it just like that. You wouldn't believe me about the man in the rose gardens. And you wouldn't listen when I told you I felt watched every time I left the house. Now someone has put a brick through the front window! Please don't try to make out there's something wrong with me because I won't treat this as normal.

MCDERMOT: I'm not asking you to treat it as normal.

FRIEDA: What's wrong, John? Are the Prods not allowed to be bad? (*She turns and picks up her case.*) I think you're becoming something of an apologist for your tribe.

(*He leaps out of bed and slaps her across the head.*)

MCDERMOT: How dare you! (*In a rage, he hits her again.*) How dare you! (*Hits her again.*) I've spent my life fighting sectarianism.

(*She falls into the corner, putting up her hands to protect her face and head. He hits out again.*)

FRIEDA: Stop it! Please!

(*He is standing over her breathing deeply, while she is crouched on the floor holding her head, unable and afraid to look up at him or move. He begins to pace the room.*)

MCDERMOT: My father was driven out of the shipyards thirty years ago. He was thrown from the deck of a ship by his workmates. When he plunged into the water he had to swim for his life; they pelted him with rivets, spanners, crowbars, anything they had to hand. His tribe, my tribe, drove him out. And they did so because he tried to set up a union. He was a Protestant and a socialist. He was unemployed most of my life. Don't ever call me an apologist for my tribe again!

(*She gets up and runs into the hall, where she bolts the door behind her. She sits down on the floor with her head in her hands and weeps.* MCDERMOT *comes to the door.*)

Frieda! Open the door!

FRIEDA: (*Voice off. Shouts.*) No! I never want to see you again.

(MCDERMOT *begins to bang his head against the door, very hard. Several times. She is so frightened by this that she gets up and opens the door.*)

Stop it! Please! Stop it!

MCDERMOT: Don't shut me out! Don't leave me!

FRIEDA: But I can't stay here any more. I can't!

MCDERMOT: If you leave me, I'll kill myself.

FRIEDA: If I stay, you'll kill me – or they will.

(*He gets up and immediately bangs his head against the door again. Alarmed, she pulls him away to restrain him.*)

All right. All right. I won't leave. But stop doing that! Please stop it!

MCDERMOT: I love you, Frieda. I'll never let you go. I love you.

(*He embraces her. She looks distressed.*)

SCENE 9

DONNA, JOSIE, DANNY, FRIEDA, MALACHY, LIAM.

Donna's living room. The room is empty. JOSIE *comes in, followed by* DONNA *who is wearing only a dressing-gown and slippers.*)

JOSIE: I haven't seen you for so long, I was worried. Were you sleeping?

DONNA: What time is it?

JOSIE: It's not that late. You're not usually in bed at this time. When I was here we used to sit up all night.

(DANNY *appears.*)

DANNY: Hello, Josie.

JOSIE: Hi.

DANNY: I'll head away on. See you later. Good night.

(He exits.)

DONNA: Are you staying? (*Pause.*) Is something wrong?

JOSIE: I'm not used to this. You might have told me!

DONNA: Like you told me about the baby?

(JOSIE *sits down.*)

JOSIE: I saw Liam at the club.

DONNA: Liam? What does he look like?

JOSIE: It's not his fault that he can't come home!

DONNA: No? But he can see other people.

JOSIE: Oh God. What a mess.

DONNA: (*Lighting a cigarette*) Next time you see him, would you give him a message from me? Would you ask him to leave me alone?

JOSIE: You don't mean that.

DONNA: I do. I'm happy with Danny. He's young, he makes me feel innocent. (*Pause.*) Why didn't you tell me about the baby?

JOSIE: I tried to once. You rushed off.

DONNA: You should have come and told me.

(DONNA *sits.*)

Did you want it?

JOSIE: I was surprised. It was a shock.

DONNA: What about Joe?

JOSIE: He's inscrutable. At first he wanted me to have an abortion so I'd be free.

DONNA: So that he could be free.

JOSIE: But now he's come around. He said he never thought he could make love to a pregnant woman.

DONNA: Is he away?

JOSIE: He's in Malta. He's due back tonight. I was too excited to sit in the house and wait on my own. And there were no women at the club, so – I felt a bit prominent.

(They both laugh.)

DONNA: Josie, I think you look beautiful. You suit a bit of weight on.

JOSIE: You know something, when he first came here, I wasn't sure about his motives. Then I realized that he had come to Ireland to win back his wife. I thought, I'm going to make this man love me.

DONNA: We all do desperate things when we're lonely.

JOSIE: (*Looking at herself*) I'll never be lonely again!

(FRIEDA *puts her head round the door*.)

FRIEDA: I was looking for a party. Did I come to the right place? (*They all stand and stare, then laugh*.)

JOSIE: Frieda!

DONNA: Look who it is! You're a stranger. (*Hugs* FRIEDA.)

FRIEDA: Look at you. (FRIEDA *hugs* JOSIE.)

JOSIE: You look great.

FRIEDA: (*To* JOSIE) You look different. It's your face; it's fatter. No, it's not – I don't know what it is.

DONNA: She's pregnant.

FRIEDA: (*Pause*.) What did my daddy say?

JOSIE: Nothing.

FRIEDA: As bad as that? He's good at saying nothing.

JOSIE: No, really. He was OK.

(DONNA *excitedly goes off to the kitchen for glasses and a bottle*.)

FRIEDA: Well, tell me this, did you marry well?

JOSIE: Who's married!

FRIEDA: Look, I'm dying to ask. Is there a father?

JOSIE: Joe Conran.

FRIEDA: I always liked him. He's kinda shy.

DONNA: (*Returning*) This calls for a celebration.

(*She pours the new wine into a glass for each one*.)

FRIEDA: I thought I saw Danny McLoughlin from the top of the street.

DONNA: You just missed him.

FRIEDA: I think I did.

DONNA: So let's have a toast.

FRIEDA: To?

DONNA: To Josie's baby . . . To Frieda's return . . . To my love!

(*They clink glasses and drink.*)

FRIEDA: Was it an accident?

DONNA: Frieda!

JOSIE: I wanted this.

FRIEDA: Did it matter who the father was?

JOSIE: I wouldn't have wanted it to be Cathal's child.

(DONNA *chokes on her wine, and looks in amazement at* JOSIE.)

JOSIE: It's all right. I can talk about it now.

FRIEDA: Sure everybody knew about you and Cathal O'Donnell. (*Drinks.*) Anyway, he's got nine kids already.

DONNA: Ten. She had a girl.

FRIEDA: She must be worn out.

DONNA: She's my age.

FRIEDA: She looks ten years older.

JOSIE: A child for every year . . . that I knew him.

DONNA: (*To* FRIEDA) What did you start!

JOSIE: I spoke to her once – a long time ago. It was just after I first saw her. She was suffering because of the heat. 'He loves children,' she said. 'He's hoping for a boy this time.' I tried to end it then.

(DONNA *pours more wine into Josie's glass.*)

DONNA: I don't think you should be drinking in your condition. (*They laugh. There is immediate hammering at the door.*) (*Springs to her feet and looks out of the window.*) That's your daddy! And you're not supposed to be here.

JOSIE: You could hide in the kitchen.

FRIEDA: No! (*She stands up with her arms folded and waits.* DONNA *lets* MALACHY *into the room. He seems in a hurry. He stops at the sight of* FRIEDA, *then turns to* JOSIE.)

MALACHY: Are you fit to travel?

JOSIE: I'm pregnant, Daddy; I'm not an invalid!

MALACHY: I've come to take you away with me now.

JOSIE: Why?

MALACHY: The *Sea Fern* was met as soon as it entered Irish waters – before the fishing fleet could get to her and before the crew could dump the cargo.

JOSIE: Who met her?

MALACHY: Irish security police – they were tipped off this afternoon by the British Government. Our contact in the Guarda said the shipment was betrayed in Valetta. The British had been following its progress since it left Malta.

JOSIE: (*Suddenly alarmed*) Jesus! God! What's happened to Joe?

MALACHY: Josie! It was Joe who betrayed us! Everybody's saying it. I've come to take you away with me.

JOSIE: Who's saying it?

MALACHY: Ask Liam.

JOSIE: Liam's down on Joe. What does Cathal say?

MALACHY: Cathal is stubborn enough to believe that Joe Conran is coming back – he insists on waiting for him at the rendezvous.

JOSIE: (*Relieved*) Believe Cathal.

MALACHY: Listen. Joe's coming back isn't proof of his innocence.

JOSIE: The capture of the *Sea Fern* is not proof of Joe's guilt. We've lost shipments before!

MALACHY: If Conran is a British agent they'll be looking for us and everyone he's met.

JOSIE: Joe would not betray me! I've lived with him. I know him. I'm carrying his child. Do you not think I would know?

(*Hammering at the door. Everyone freezes.*)

DONNA: (*Looks out of the window.*) Liam.

MALACHY: Go on, girl. Open the door!

(DONNA *moves quickly to the door, admitting* LIAM.)

What's happened, son?

LIAM: (*Starts suddenly at the sight of* FRIEDA.) What's she doing here?

MALACHY: Who?

LIAM: Frieda! She's standing right behind you!

MALACHY: I don't see anyone. What's wrong, for Christ's sake!

LIAM: Gabriel drove out of the hospital tonight with a van load of supplies. He was stopped by the police. He showed them his forged security pass and told them he was delivering provisions to the Nurses' Home.

MALACHY: At this time of night?

LIAM: They let him go. He drove the stuff straight to the club as usual.

MALACHY: What – the pin head!

LIAM: Of course, he didn't know the police were following him. They arrested him and everybody on the premises for handling stolen goods. O'Donnell was among the people arrested. (*Slightly turning in* DONNA*'s way and then back.*) So was that musician, Danny McLoughlin. He'd just walked in.

MALACHY: Holy Jesus!

(DONNA *crosses the room to where* JOSIE *is standing.*)

DONNA: How come you got away?

LIAM: I wasn't on the premises.

JOSIE: How do you know all this?

LIAM: Eileen Watterson told me. She's a barmaid at the club.

MALACHY: Now do you believe me?

JOSIE: This is pure chance!

LIAM: It was a cover for a raid.

JOSIE: Joe would not betray me!

LIAM: He's not coming back!

JOSIE: I don't believe it.

LIAM: Josie. He got what he came for. Eileen told me they went straight to O'Donnell. They even had a layout of the club. And they knew what he looked like.

JOSIE: No. No. No!

LIAM: How many months pregnant are you?

JOSIE: Three.

LIAM: Kill it. I want you to kill the child!

JOSIE: Why?

LIAM: The father is a traitor. He did not love you; he used you. It's better that his child should not be born at all.

JOSIE: But it's my baby – it doesn't matter about anything else.

LIAM: It's his child!

DONNA: No. It's not, Liam. It's what you never understood. A child doesn't belong to anyone. It's itself.

(LIAM *grabs* JOSIE*'s arms.*)

LIAM: Do it. Don't force us!

JOSIE: (*In terror*) No!

MALACHY: Take your hands off her!

(LIAM *lets go of* JOSIE*'s arm*)

MALACHY: I'm the father here, son!

LIAM: What's wrong with you? She's carrying Conran's baby!

(MALACHY *puts his arm round* JOSIE.)

MALACHY: My baby now. (*Pause while he looks around.*) Josie's going to live with me from now on. Isn't that right, love?

JOSIE: (*Hesitant*) Yes.

MALACHY: This baby's my blood. If anyone harms a hair on its head. . . !

LIAM: You're an old man, Malachy.

(MALACHY *begins to move through the room to the door, leading* JOSIE *away with him.*)

MALACHY: I'll live twice as long as you, son!

(MALACHY *opens the door.*)

Now Josie and I are going to take a wee trip away from all this attention – I advise you three to do the same. The soldiers will be here before long.

(*He leads* JOSIE *away.*)

DONNA: Josie!

(*She does not turn round. They exit.*)

LIAM: I have to make tracks.

(LIAM *prepares to leave.*)

DONNA: Liam!

LIAM: I can't stay, Donna. They'll be looking for me. I couldn't go back in there.

DONNA: I'll be here.

LIAM: I'd prefer if she wasn't!

FRIEDA: I came to say goodbye to my sisters, I wasn't intending to stay.

DONNA: (*To* LIAM) Come back when it's safe.

(LIAM *appears to want to embrace* DONNA, *but she isn't encouraging. He thinks better of it, and leaves quickly.*)

FRIEDA: Why don't you leave him!

(They sit on the sofa.)

DONNA: *(Mildly surprised)* Why? How?

FRIEDA: You're not happy.

DONNA: I think I may have lost the capacity for happiness. I left my son for him. I thought if I had another it would make it up. But it didn't. As soon as I conceived I noticed the change. I lost my desire. All my life I felt I had to run fast, seek, look, struggle for things and hold on to things or lose them, but as soon as I felt the child inside me again, the baby quickening, I knew that it was coming and there was nothing I could do. I felt for the first time the course of things, the inevitability. And I thought, no, I won't struggle any more, I shall just do. And all that time – longing – was wasted, because life just turns things out as they are. Happiness, sadness, has really nothing to do with it.

(A child begins to cry upstairs. DONNA *listens.* FRIEDA *makes a move to go.)*

DONNA: Don't go yet.

FRIEDA: I'll stay until it's light.

(The crying stops. The room darkens.)

DONNA: She has wee dreams. I'll bring her down if she cries again. *(Pause.)* So you're saying goodbye.

FRIEDA: *(Nods.)* I left him sleeping. I walked out just as I am. If I'd taken a suitcase he'd have known and stopped me.

DONNA: Have you somewhere to go?

FRIEDA: England.

DONNA: Why England?

FRIEDA: Why not? It's my language.

DONNA: Why not go South?

FRIEDA: I'm not that kind of Irish.

DONNA: It didn't work out then?

FRIEDA: No.

DONNA: Any reason?

FRIEDA: Different commitments.

DONNA: It'll be lonely.

FRIEDA: I'd rather be lonely than suffocate.

DONNA: I understand, but it only lasts a little while that feeling. As you get older, companionship is very important. Filling the space in the bed with someone. Preferably a good friend.

FRIEDA: I want to write songs.

DONNA: Write to me.

FRIEDA: If I have anything to say. (*Pause. Looks away from* DONNA *straight ahead.*) I remember a long time ago, a moonlit night on a beach below the Mournes, we were having a late summer barbecue on the shore at Tyrella. Among the faces at the fire were Josie, Donna, Liam, and my father and mother were there too. And John McDermot was a friend of Liam's.

DONNA: I remember.

FRIEDA: We three slipped off from the campfire to swim leaving the men arguing on the beach. And Donna said. 'I'm going to marry Liam McCoy one day.' And we all laughed. And I said, 'Well then, I'll marry John McDermot.' And we sank down into the calm water and tried to catch the phosphorescence on the surface of the waves – it was the first time I'd ever seen it – and the moon was reflected on the sea that night. It was as though we swam in the night sky and cupped the stars between our cool fingers. And then they saw us. First Liam and then John, and my father in a temper because we'd left our swimsuits on the beach. And the shouting and the slapping and the waves breaking over us. We raced for cover to another part of the shore. We escaped into the shadows and were clothed again before they reached us. We lay down in the sandhills and laughed.

DONNA: I remember.

FRIEDA: I have not thought of that night for many years.

DONNA: (*Looking out*) The sky's getting lighter.

FRIEDA: Oh, it's not him; it is Ireland I am leaving.

DONNA: How quietly the light comes.

(*Darkness.*)

THE LONG MARCH

For my mother and father

CHARACTERS

HELEN WALSH
JOE WALSH
ROSE WALSH
FRANK MOLLOY
BRIDIE MOLLOY
COLM
FERGUS SLOAN
CASSANDRA SLOAN
MICHAEL CANNING
MONA O'HARE
MRS MCCOY
FATHER OLIVER

The play covers the period from 30 March 1979 to 18 December 1980, and is set between West Belfast and Stranmillis.

The Long March was first shown on BBC1 Television on 20 November 1984. The cast was as follows:

HELEN WALSH	Marcella Riordan
JOE WALSH	James Ellis
ROSE WALSH	Doreen Hepburn
FRANK MOLLOY	Louis Rolston
BRIDIE MOLLOY	Leila Webster
COLM	Adrian Dunbar
FERGUS SLOAN	Tony Doyle
CASSANDRA SLOAN	Valerie Lilley
MICHAEL CANNING	Ciaran Hinds
MONA O'HARE	Emer Gillespie
MRS MCCOY	Catherine Gibson
FATHER OLIVER	Denys Hawthorne
Producer	Keith Williams
Director	Chris Parr
Camera	John Otterson
Lighting	Stan Snape
Designer	John Armstrong

1. BLANK SCREEN WITH VOICE-OVER TANNOY ANNOUNCEMENT:

[*Superimpose title*]
'The 21.30 to Holyhead, the Irish Mail, will leave from platform five calling at Crewe and Holyhead. This train conveys sleeping car accommodation, and a buffet car, and connects with the 03.15 Sealink service to Dun Laoghaire.'

2. EXT. DAY. 10.00 AM.

Aerial or overhead view of the back of the City Hall. Superimpose caption: Belfast 30 March 1979.
Move down in on back gate. JOE WALSH'*s car is leaving. Close up to pavement level. The uniformed* SECURITY MAN *at the gate waves him on. He turns right into the one-way traffic keeping close to the edge of the pavement. He is watched by the* SECURITY MAN *and a stray cat that has made its home inside the City Hall gates.* JOE *immediately stops his car on the double yellow lines, puts on both indicators and takes out a newspaper to read while waiting:* ROSE *is late. The* SECURITY MAN *stoops to the cat.* ROSE *hurries along the pavement.* JOE *crumples his newspaper, puts it away and starts the engine almost before she has got into the front passenger seat. The car follows the one-way traffic: a long shot up Howard Street, and Grosvenor Road to the Black Mountain, before Joe's car turns towards the front of the City Hall in the direction of Central Station.*

3. EXT. BELFAST CENTRAL STATION. DAY. 10.20 AM.

Fade up station sounds. Long shot of a busy station platform. ROSE *and* JOE *are waiting for a train to arrive. They are facing an Arrivals Board with various named Irish towns – significantly Dublin.* HELEN'*s parents,* ROSE *and* JOE, *look remarkably similar, from a distance.* ROSE *is the same width and height as* JOE. *They are comfortably dressed.* MRS WALSH *pays particular attention to her dress.* ROSE *gasps at the sight of her daughter.*

ROSE: There she is now, Joe.

(HELEN *is suddenly visible after the other passengers have moved on, she appears quite alone. A* PORTER *is coming along behind her, pushing a trunk and three suitcases on a broken trolley, the only one he could find. Close up on Helen's face. She looks quite distressed, but has her emotions under control. She appears to stop for a moment at the sight of her parents.*)

JOE: I could kill him.

ROSE: (*Suppressing emotion*) You can't take sides!

4. INT. LIVING ROOM. WALSHS' HOUSE. ST JAMES ROAD. DAY. 6.00 PM.

Later the same day. Living room of Rose and Joe Walsh's house in St James Road. A large close up of a seating arrangement for a wedding reception. A hand is printing in the names on either side of the bride and groom.

HELEN: (*Coming into the room*) I put the other suitcase on the landing. I hope it won't be in the way.

(HELEN *is dressed to go out.*)

ROSE: (*Looking up from her task*) Where are you off to?

HELEN: I'm expecting Michael at any minute.

ROSE: Michael Canning? His girlfriend's a model.

HELEN: I'm sure she is.

ROSE: (*Focusing on her task again*) I don't know what I'm going to do about these place names. Are you going to be here for the wedding?

HELEN: Well, I'm going to be here for a while.

ROSE: You picked a fine time to leave your husband with your sister getting married next month.

(*Medium close up of* HELEN)

HELEN: I'm sorry.

ROSE: (*Staring inconsolably at the table which is full of invitation cards, magazines, papers, dress patterns for bridesmaids, scraps of material and menu cards*) I wish you'd given me some warning. You told me you wouldn't be at the wedding.

HELEN: (*Coming to sit at the table with her* MOTHER) I'm sorry.

ROSE: I don't know where I'm going to put you!

HELEN: Look, I can't go on saying I'm sorry any more.

(*They stare at each other in silence.*)

Why don't you just count me out?

ROSE: (*Repentant*) Don't be ridiculous. What are you planning to do now?

(*Helen's attention is caught by a copy of* Fortnight *with four blanket women on the front.*)

HELEN: Get a job.

(*She picks it up. Underneath is a copy of the magazine* Brides.)

ROSE: I'll have to put you next to Mrs McCoy. There isn't room at the top table. And listen, if Sadie McCoy asks you where Cliff is, you're to say that only one of you could come.

(HELEN *lets the paper drop back on top of the other. Gets up from the table.*)

HELEN: (*Quietly, to herself almost.*) Oh Mummy, why tell lies!

ROSE: What sort of job are you getting?

HELEN: Michael has offered me a research job on a book he's writing with Fergus Sloan.

(ROSE *turns to* HELEN, *almost in panic.*)

ROSE: Fergus Sloan! Is that why you've come back! Fergus Sloan is married now.

HELEN: Oh Rose!

ROSE: (*Getting up from the table and following her*) Don't you Oh Rose me! I'm your mother. I don't know what you're doing here or why you've left Cliff and I'm not going to ask. Mind you I never thought he was very good to you – but I never take sides. I know only too well what you're like.

(HELEN *sighs.*)

That fellow Fergus Sloan's at it again – writing to the *Irish Times* supporting the H-Block protest. Did you know that?

HELEN: Yes. Mummy, he's a lawyer. It is his job.

ROSE: Aye. He is. And it's easy to be romantic about the Provos when you live in Stranmillis!

(HELEN *looks down in silence.*)

I'm tired of it. I'm sick and I'm tired of it. And your father's just as bad. He can take his bed to the City Hall as far as I'm concerned. He's never out of it. (*Looks at the littered table.*) He hasn't lifted a finger for this wedding. He's even organized a conference for the same weekend. I told him: 'Joe, you can't do that. Pauline's getting married.' He said: 'I know . . .'

(JOE WALSH *opens the front door into the hall.* ROSE *suddenly reacts; the rest of what she is saying trails away. Loudly*) That's your father now. He's early for a change.

(JOE *comes into the room.*)

HELEN: (*Quickly smiling*) Hello, Daddy. Did your meeting go all right?

(*He stares back in silence at the two women.*)

ROSE: What's wrong? There's something wrong, isn't there?

JOE: Airey Neave's been murdered. His car was blown up in the House of Commons car park. Thatcher's cracked up on television. And Fitt's just called the Provos bastards.

ROSE: Oh God save us! What next?

(JOE *sits down heavily on the sofa.*)

JOE: Can you get me some tea? I've got to go out again.

(ROSE *goes immediately to the kitchen which is the opposite end of the room from the door.* HELEN *sits down with her* FATHER.)

HELEN: Who killed Neave?

JOE: Well, Fitt obviously thinks it was the Provos.

HELEN: But why?

JOE: Why? Do you ask me why?

HELEN: Why Neave? Mason is the Secretary of State.

JOE: Not for much longer. The Labour Party's going to lose this election. Callaghan's thrown it away.

ROSE: (*Coming out of the kitchen*) Do you want a fry?

JOE: Aye, anything you have, Rose.

(*She retreats again.*)

Fitt went to see him after the Bennett Report came out, to complain about Mason saying ill-treatment hadn't taken place. Imagine a Labour Minister supporting interrogation centres. But would the Prime Minister talk about it? Not at all. Callaghan walked him round the library in 10 Downing Street, showed him the carpets and the nice prints and the furnishings and said: 'Would you look at this, Gerry. Gladstone sat here. Think of the tradition!' And Thatcher will be sitting there come the fourth of May, thanks to him. Neave is the Shadow Secretary of State. That's why he was killed.

(ROSE *comes out of the kitchen again with a piece of frozen meat in Cellophane. She holds it up to* JOE.)

ROSE: I could do you a frozen steak grilled. It would be better for you.

JOE: Whatever you like, Rose.

(*She retreats again.*)

The irony is . . .

(*Sound of doorbell;* HELEN *reacts, turns her head.* JOE *continues.*)

. . . Neave went on telly to say he accepted Bennett's recommendations and he would end the interrogation centres if the Conservatives got in.

(HELEN *gets up quickly.*)

HELEN: Hang on. That's probably Michael for me.

(JOE WALSH *sits listening to the scene in the hall.*)

MICHAEL: (*Voice over*) Helen! It's great to see you.

HELEN: (*Voice over*) I'll not kiss you or I'll get lipstick all over your face.

MICHAEL: (*Voice over*) You're thinner. I can feel your ribs.

HELEN: (*Voice over*) Come on in for a minute.

(JOE *gets to his feet as they come into the room.* ROSE *joins them from the kitchen.*)

MICHAEL: Oh hello, Mrs Walsh, Joe.

ROSE: (*Nods.*) Michael.

JOE: Hello, Michael. How are things at the university?

MICHAEL: Fine. How are things with you? I haven't seen you for a long time.

ROSE: Sure, you saw us last week at the Europa, but you didn't know us.

(HELEN *raises her eyes to the ceiling.* MICHAEL *looks ahead, embarrassed.* JOE *looks at* ROSE.)

5. EXT. ST JAMES ROAD. DAY. (*Continuous*)

MICHAEL *and* HELEN *are walking up St James Road towards the Falls.*

MICHAEL: That was tense. What happened?
HELEN: Airey Neave's been murdered.
MICHAEL: Yes. I heard. It's a hell of a business!
HELEN: There's also the fact that my sister is getting married next month. I've just left my husband. And you and Fergus Sloan and the Civil Rights marchers are responsible for all our troubles. But the real trouble is my father is never at home.

6. INT. DAY. 6.15 PM.

ROSE *is setting the table, or a part of it, for Joe's evening meal.* JOE *is watching her.*

JOE: What was all that about?
ROSE: She's always the same. She doesn't care about anyone but herself.
JOE: I wonder why she came back.
(ROSE *picks up some new pale-green towels.*)
ROSE: You know I don't like the colour of these towels she's given Pauline as a wedding present. I think I'll try and change them.
JOE: Did she say anything to you?
ROSE: (*Shakes her head.*) She lives on another planet, that Helen. Another planet entirely.
JOE: Aye. England.

7. EXT. FALLS ROAD. DAY. 6.15 PM.

HELEN *and* MICHAEL *leave St James Road and cross to the opposite side of the Falls Road, to the corner of the Whiterock*

Road. Behind them the slogans on the wall mark the changing strength of opinions during the H-Block protest.
In white lettering on this day it reads: 'Support the blanket men.'

MICHAEL: It's like I said, Fergus is writing a book on punishment. I've been helping him with the historical part, but he needs someone else with a legal background to go through the law reports. I'm afraid it's a rather laborious task. Nothing exciting.

HELEN: I don't mind that. I haven't worked for a long time. Is Fergus doing anything on the H-Block issue in this book?

MICHAEL: No!

HELEN: Why not?

MICHAEL: Because we're looking at the ordinary courts, not the special courts.

HELEN: But it's still punishment!

(HELEN *is watching out for a taxi.*)

MICHAEL: It's a book for students everywhere. It's not particularly related to Northern Ireland.

HELEN: That's absurd. How can you write about the prison system and not refer to the Maze?

(HELEN *waves down a taxi.*)

MICHAEL: Could we not get a bus?

HELEN: A black taxi is quicker and cheaper.

MICHAEL: The Provos run those taxis!

(*The taxi stops.*)

I don't like colluding with illegality!

HELEN: Michael!

(*She looks wearily at him and gets in. He follows. The taxi moves off.*)

8. EXT. DAY. 6.20 PM.

The taxi journey along the Falls Road as seen from the pavement and above in traffic.

MICHAEL: (*Voice over*) How did Joe and your mother take your arrival in Belfast?

HELEN: (*Voice over*) Rose burst into tears. Joe overtipped the porter and asked him if he was in a union. (*Sighs.*)

(*Continue scenes of the Falls Road and of the taxi travelling along it. Graffiti of the period is evident on certain landmarks such as the red brick wall of the Royal Victoria Hospital.*)

God Almighty! I forget how suffocating this place can be. Then I'm not back five minutes before it hits me. How do you survive?

MICHAEL: (*Voice over*) My girlfriend lives in Dublin. I escape there every weekend. She's a model. She's not the least bit interested in politics.

(*Shots of the Falls Road, passing Divis Flats.*)

HELEN: (*Voice over*) Lucky lady.

9. EXT. CASTLE STREET. DAY. 6.25 PM.

MICHAEL *and* HELEN *get out of the taxi.* HELEN, *who has been away for some time, stops to look down Castle Street towards the security gates, where the taxis turn and come to a halt. Helen's point of view: there are queues of taxis and people, also street traders at barrows, the city centre can be seen through the gates. She turns and walks off with* MICHAEL *in the direction of Great Victoria Street, towards Stranmillis.*

10. EXT. DAY. 6.40 PM.

An elderly man in a cap, FRANK MOLLOY, *is passing along a terrace of elegant double-fronted bay-windowed houses in a quiet cul-de-sac, in Stranmillis. He stops and checks a piece of paper. Then walks on to the end of the row.*

11. INT. THE SITTING ROOM/STUDY OF FERGUS SLOAN'S HOUSE IN STRANMILLIS. DAY.

He is sitting at a table with a typewriter and several law reports in front of him. There is also a Dictaphone on the table. He is not typing, and not reading, but has his head in his hands and is staring ahead.

CASSANDRA: (*Voice over*) Fergus! I'm going now. Fergus!
(FERGUS *closes his eyes when she first calls his name, and finally responds.*)

FERGUS: Right.
(*She comes into the study.*)

CASSANDRA: You look terrible. You said to waken you before I went out. I suppose you'll be up half the night again on that book.

FERGUS: I've got a chapter to finish.

CASSANDRA: You've always got a chapter to finish. Did you sleep at all?

FERGUS: Yes. Between five and six.

CASSANDRA: Do you think we could talk some time?

FERGUS: Well, not just at the moment. Michael's coming and I've got a lot to do.

CASSANDRA: I said, some time.

FERGUS: Yes. All right.

CASSANDRA: I'm taking Simon to my mother's for the weekend. He's waiting in the car.
(*No response from* FERGUS.)
I'd better go.
(*She walks out, slamming the door.*)

FERGUS: Cassandra! Oh damn. (*He slams the typewriter carriage across in front of him, and looks at the pile of papers on his desk. A slight, nervous knock at the door. Turns, startled.*) Yes?
(FRANK *opens the door and comes into the room.*)

FRANK: Excuse me. Sorry to startle you. I met your wife outside. She told me to come on in.
(FERGUS *has got to his feet.* MOLLOY *has taken his cap off and is holding it in his hands.*)
My name's Frank Molloy. I'm from Andersonstown.

FERGUS: (*Indicating*) Sit down, Mr Molloy. What can I do for you?

FRANK: You don't know me, Mr Sloan. The solicitor suggested

I come and see you. He gave me your address.

(FERGUS *has gone to the fireplace to pick up his pipe.*)

FERGUS: Yes?

FRANK: (*Struggling*) Well – I have three sons in Long Kesh, but it's Brendan, my youngest, I'm worried about. He's on the blanket.

(FERGUS *turns his attention from filling the pipe to* FRANK MOLLOY'*s face.*)

What I mean to say is, I read your article in the paper about the protest. I thought it was very good.

FERGUS: Thank you. But I don't really see what –

FRANK: It said in the newspaper you were doing a book on prisons, on punishment, so, well – I represent some of the relatives of the men on the blanket and we thought that if more people like you could put pressure on the government we might get our demands.

(FERGUS *has walked to his desk chair to sit down, having lit the pipe.* FRANK'*s gaze follows him.*)

If I could be of help with information, I'd be glad to let you meet the other relatives and some of the boys who've been released.

FERGUS: (*Puts his pipe down.*) I'm sorry, there's been a misunderstanding; this book isn't about the protest. It's historical. I'm an academic. I only lecture in politics.

FRANK: Oh, I see. You mean you're not writing anything about the H-Blocks.

FERGUS: No.

FRANK: I thought from what you said in your article you were trying to change the situation in the Kesh.

FERGUS: Well, I am, of course. But those two things are separate. The book and the article.

FRANK: I see. There's been talk that maybe the Human Rights Court might be able to help us. We won there before.

FERGUS: Yes. I gathered that was happening. In fact I know some of the solicitors involved. Mr Molloy, I have to make it clear now – I'm not in sympathy with the Provos – not with their politics. In that article I was taking a humanitarian stand.

FRANK: Och sure, I know that.

(*Pause. Looks down at his cap which he is twisting in his hands.*) Do you have a son, Mr Sloan?

FERGUS: (*A little unsure now*) I have. Yes. He's six.

FRANK: Well, if your son was on the dirty protest, I don't suppose you could stand by.

FERGUS: No. I don't suppose I would.

(FRANK MOLLOY *gets up, so does* FERGUS.)

FRANK: I'd better be off. If you do decide to help us, come and talk to me about it.

FERGUS: I will. Good luck with the campaign.

FRANK: You're a brave man, anyway, putting your name to that piece. I remember you with the students making a speech on television a lot of years ago. It was outside the University with the Civil Rights Marchers. Those were the days.

12. EXT. STRANMILLIS ROAD. DAY. 6.55 PM.

HELEN *and* MICHAEL *are passing a small greystone church, then turning into the quiet cul-de-sac. They will approach Fergus's house confidently because they know the way.*

HELEN: Did you see his article in the *Irish Times*?

MICHAEL: He was asked to write it.

HELEN: What did you think of it?

MICHAEL: I didn't agree with its conclusions. I don't support Special Category status.

HELEN: But if they've got Special Courts they ought to have Special Category status. There's no reason why not.

MICHAEL: That's the Provo line.

HELEN: Is it? That's the trouble with living in England – you never know whose line you've got.

(*Pause.* HELEN *seems nervous.*)

What did Fergus say when you told him about me helping?

MICHAEL: I haven't told him.

HELEN: What?

(FRANK MOLLOY *passes them.*)

MICHAEL: I thought you could tell him yourself.

HELEN: Michael! (*She stops.*) Fergus hasn't seen me in ten years. And I'm supposed to go along now and ask him for a job!

MICHAEL: It'll be all right; he'll be delighted to see you.

(MICHAEL *grabs* HELEN'*s arm as she seems on the point of running away.*)

HELEN: Cassandra won't.

(*They walk on towards the door.*)

MICHAEL: Oh yes, Cassandra. She's not being very supportive just now.

13. INT. LIVING ROOM/STUDY OF FERGUS'S HOUSE. DAY.

FERGUS *is typing, then stops, and types again, and stops. He continues to stare at the paper on the typewriter before him.*

MICHAEL: (*Voice over*) Fergus! Fergus! (*Comes into the room.*)

FERGUS: Oh Michael.

MICHAEL: The front door's open to the world! Are you all right?

FERGUS: Yes. I'm struggling with a sentence here.

MICHAEL: You look as if you've seen a ghost.

FERGUS: No.

MICHAEL: You're on your own, are you?

FERGUS: Yes. Cass has gone to her mother's. Have you brought the tables?

MICHAEL: No. Not yet.

FERGUS: I thought you were bringing them with you.

MICHAEL: I brought you something else instead.

FERGUS: Oh?

MICHAEL: Remember we agreed there was some money in the budget to pay for a research assistant?

FERGUS: Have you found someone?

MICHAEL: I think I have.

FERGUS: What's his background?

MICHAEL: Actually it's a lady and she has a law degree.

FERGUS: Is she from Belfast?

MICHAEL: Yes.

FERGUS: Where's she from?

MICHAEL: (*Resisting*) From Belfast.

FERGUS: Michael!

MICHAEL: West Belfast.

FERGUS: (*Turning away*) It's out of the question.

MICHAEL: (*Angry*) Now wait a minute. You're a Catholic, or do you think a Protestant wife gives you immunity?

FERGUS: No. You wait a minute. You know very well that for every piece of work done here the Director of Public Prosecutions, the press and every fringe organization with an axe to grind has a whole team of operators working to dig up the dirt on the authors. With one Catholic author and one Protestant, this research is what you might call balanced and I'm not about to jeopardize it.

(MICHAEL, *who has been standing over* FERGUS *now turns away*.)

MICHAEL: For God's sake, Fergus! She's only a research assistant; it isn't as though she's a senior author. (*Changing his tone and turning back*) She needs a job badly, and she is a friend of mine.

FERGUS: What are her politics?

MICHAEL: She's not mixed up with anybody. Not as far as I know.

FERGUS: Non-aligned, and comes from West Belfast?

MICHAEL: She's been away – living in England, Leeds mainly, and recently London.

FERGUS: All right. I'll see her on Monday at my office.

MICHAEL: Well, actually, she's outside. I thought you could see her now.

FERGUS: Oh you haven't. Not now.

MICHAEL: I won't be a minute.

(*He leaves quickly.* FERGUS *looks in despair at the piece of paper in front of him.*)

FERGUS: Damn!

(*He rips it from the machine, and gets up as* MICHAEL *returns. He turns to face* MICHAEL *and* HELEN. MICHAEL *is gripping* HELEN *by the arm. She looks as if she's likely to run away from the scene at any moment.*)

MICHAEL: I think you two know each other.

(*Slight pause:* FERGUS *stares at* HELEN, *a young woman with long hair, wearing a white sheepskin jacket.*)

HELEN: Hello, Fergus.

FERGUS: Good God.

(*Looks at* MICHAEL.)

Michael –

MICHAEL: Yes. I'm on my way. I'll pick up the tables from the computer centre right now.

FERGUS: Michael! Wait a minute!

(*He slams the door behind him.*)

HELEN: (*Feigned cheerfulness*) Oh dear. He doesn't change.

FERGUS: (*Extremely hostile*) What are you doing here?

HELEN: Michael told me there was a job to do, and that I'd be welcome.

(*Pause. No encouragement from* FERGUS.)

I'm sorry to have intruded on you. I'll go.

FERGUS: Oh for God's sake! Don't you rush off as well. What are you doing here?

HELEN: Please don't misunderstand this. I'm not looking for anything from you except, perhaps – direction.

(FERGUS *sits down at the end of the desk/table and watches her.*)

FERGUS: I saw your wedding in the paper about eight years ago.

HELEN: I saw yours.

FERGUS: How is he? Your – history lecturer.

(HELEN *has her hands in her pockets. She looks at her feet and then raises her head.*)

HELEN: He's not with me.

FERGUS: Just like that. You always did walk away from anything that didn't suit you.

HELEN: You could give me the benefit of the doubt on this occasion. I didn't want to. I had no choice.

FERGUS: That's what you told me.

HELEN: Fergus, please.

FERGUS: Why did you leave him?

HELEN: I needed to come back. I haven't been well. I haven't worked for some time. This was Michael's idea. We kept in touch.

FERGUS: He never told me.

(*He gets up to look for his pipe among the papers on the table.*)

HELEN: I was afraid at first. This place is so small. I was afraid I'd be tripping over everyone I ever knew. Each of us wondering what we'd done in the last ten years. And nothing in the present ever matching up to what there was in the past. (*Pause.*) Do you remember the night at the PD meeting when Bernadette said: 'Mr Chairman, I will accept responsibility for the march tomorrow. I am an orphan. I have nothing to lose'? And a political campaign was born. God, I even remember what I was thinking at the moment.

FERGUS: What were you thinking?

HELEN: You were sitting right next to me. I thought, I wish I had nothing to lose.

FERGUS: You should try to stop remembering. Those days are past.

HELEN: Oh, I know that. But there are still things to be done. I read your book.

FERGUS: Which one?

HELEN: *Terrorism and the Democratic Ideal.*

FERGUS: It's all I can hope to do now. Raise the level of awareness beyond the point of a gun.

HELEN: I saw that article in the *Irish Times* about the H-Block protest. I think it's the best thing you've written. (FERGUS *is irritated.*) Are you going to do anything on H-Block in this book on punishment?

(FERGUS *gives* HELEN *a long, hard look.*)

FERGUS: Why?

HELEN: Because you have to. Because you care. Because you've written the article. And because it's a challenge. You're frightened of it. And I know you with fear – you always grab what you're afraid of. In case it gets you first.

FERGUS: Oh don't *you* tell me I'm a brave man.

HELEN: You're not – you ran away from me.

(MICHAEL *approaches, calling out from the hall.*)

MICHAEL: (*Voice over*) I'm back.

(*The door opens. We see* FERGUS *and* HELEN *from* MICHAEL*'s point of view.*)

Does she get the job?

(*He comes towards* FERGUS *and puts his arm around* HELEN.)

I've got the tables.

(*He is holding computer printouts.*)

I'm going to give them to you if you tell me she's got the job.

FERGUS: What job?

MICHAEL: The research assistant.

(FERGUS *moves to his desk to write on a pad.*)

FERGUS: Oh that. She can have that if she wants it.

(*Finishes scribbling on the pad.*)

But listen. There is something else. I want you to find a man for me.

MICHAEL: What are we doing now, keeping a balance of the sexes?

FERGUS: He's the man who walked out of here tonight. He's called Frank Molloy and he has a son in the Maze – or maybe three. Anyway, he lives in Andersonstown and I want you to find him for me and give him this note. Will you do that?

MICHAEL: (*Growing annoyance*) I thought we weren't getting into this Maze business.

FERGUS: We're not. I am. I'm going to try and help the campaign by writing a pamphlet solely on the H-Block protest.

(HELEN *is smiling.*)

MICHAEL: Is that wise?

HELEN: Ah wisdom!

MICHAEL: I mean, apart from anything else – who's going to publish it?

FERGUS: Let me worry about the publisher. In the meantime I

want you to find Frank Molloy. What I'd like to do is talk to the relatives and also, if possible, talk to the prisoners on the blanket, or any who have just been released.
(*To* HELEN) I want you to interview the women. They'll probably find it easier to talk to you. Perhaps Michael or I could get statements from the men.

MICHAEL: Count me out.
(*He looks at both their resolute faces.*)
No! I am not getting involved in this.

14. EXT. ANDERSONSTOWN. MORNING. 11.00 AM.

Sunday morning, 1 April 1979. Chapel bells in the distance, also the sound of a helicopter. HELEN *and* MICHAEL *are walking along a narrow path passing a row of houses on one side and a steep bank with a hedge on the other. This is Upper Shaws Road, the approach to Lenadoon.*

MICHAEL: If my mother knew I was on this road she'd have a fit!

HELEN: Why?

MICHAEL: She's at Stormont Golf Club this morning – playing golf with the Chief of Police.

HELEN: Do you think everyone who lives in Andersonstown is a Provo?

MICHAEL: We're not looking for everyone. (*Pause.*) Though we could be: Frank Molloy, Andersonstown, with a son in the Maze, maybe three. A unique biography. How much time do we have to find him – a year?
(*The path has ended and opened into a clearing, a small green before a row of houses, with a view over the industrial valley of Belfast.*)

HELEN: Oh stop grumbling.

MICHAEL: If this isn't it, I give up.

HELEN: (*Turns to him, smiling.*) You know something. I'm really happy again.

MICHAEL: You'll get over it.

15. INT. FRANK AND BRIDIE MOLLOY'S HOUSE. DAY.

BRIDIE *opens the door of the living room where* FRANK *is sitting reading the Sunday papers. On the wooden mantelpiece of an electric fire stand a harp, a Celtic cross and a plaque of Connolly and Pearse carved in wood.*

BRIDIE: Frankie. Here's somebody for you.
FRANK: (*Putting the paper down and getting up*) For me?
(MICHAEL *and* HELEN *approach;* BRIDIE *watches.*)
MICHAEL: I have a letter for you from Fergus Sloan. I think you know what it's about.
BRIDIE: Well, if you don't need me for a minute, I'll get on with my washing. (*To* HELEN) That's a lovely coat you've on. Is it hard to keep clean?
HELEN: Yes. (*Embarrassed*) Thank you.
(FRANK *has been reading the note, and looks up.*)
FRANK: Put the kettle on, Bridie. So he's going to write a pamphlet.
MICHAEL: Yes. And he'd like to see you at his office on Monday morning.
FRANK: (*Nodding*) Where's his office?
MICHAEL: It's in the Politics Department. The address is at the top of that bit of paper.
FRANK: Do you know I haven't been up to the university not since the time when the students went marching. (*Suddenly aware of them standing uneasily*) Here miss, sit down.
HELEN: Thank you.
FRANK: (*To* MICHAEL) You too. You'd think I owed you money the way you're standing about.
(*They sit down with relief, but are not confident enough to react to his humour.*)
What did you say your names were?
HELEN: I'm Helen. This is Michael.
MICHAEL: (*Quickly*) Are all your sons in the H-Block protest?
FRANK: No. Only Brendan. The other two have done their stint.

HELEN: What was his sentence?

FRANK: Twenty-six years for possession of firearms. He's twenty-one. (*Catching Helen's expression, and smiling*) Oh, he's not innocent.

(*The door opens. We see the three sitting in the living room from this angle.*)

I thought you were away out.

(*We now see* COLM *from the point of view of the other three. He is standing by the kitchen door, a young man in his early twenties.*)

This is Colm, my nephew. He lives with us. (COLM *moves across the room to sit by* HELEN *while* FRANK *is talking.*) The house is empty these days. And his mother has six of her own.

HELEN: Hello.

FRANK: (*To* MICHAEL) My other two sons are married, you know. So they have their own women to worry about them. But Brendan doesn't have anyone but us.

HELEN: What do you do, Colm?

(*Close up on* COLM.)

COLM: (*Spoken absolutely without humour*) Me? Oh, I work for the *Sunday Times*. I'm a photographer.

HELEN: (*She nearly believes him.*) A – are you?

FRANK: Buckin' ejeet! Of course he doesn't. They're all unemployed round here. Where are you from yourself? You don't sound Belfast. I can't quite place your voice.

COLM: She sounds mid-Atlantic to me.

HELEN: I am from Belfast, but I've lived in England for a long time.

COLM: I pity you. How can you live in England?

HELEN: Oh, it's not so bad. You only see the troops on the streets or Maggie Thatcher on the telly and you think that's England. But it's not. It's not all there is to England.

COLM: It's enough for me. I wouldn't want to know it. It must be a prison. Unless of course you work for the *Sunday Times*.

FRANK: Take no notice of him, Helen. He's a sarky pup.

HELEN: I don't, actually. I've been unemployed too.

COLM: That's very depressing. If you can't get a job with your fancy voice and that coat, there's not much hope for me.

FRANK: Och away you on. Away and chase yourself if you can't be civil.

COLM: (*Drags himself out of the seat.*) I'm away out. I don't see much to keep me here.

(*He crosses the room to the door to leave.*)

FRANK: Here! (*He gets up to follow him.*) If you're going home tell your daddy I'll be round later.

MICHAEL: (*Whispering to* HELEN) I'm glad you didn't tell him you were a research assistant and I was a university lecturer; he'd have annihilated us! (HELEN *smiles.*)

FRANK: (*Returning, having closed the door on* COLM) He doesn't know what to do with himself, that wee fellow. It's very sad.

HELEN: He's not one of the boys, then?

FRANK: Now what would you know about the boys, Helen?

HELEN: I'm very well acquainted with the terminology of West Belfast, Mr Molloy. My father and mother live off the Falls Road.

FRANK: What's your surname?

HELEN: Walsh. My father's Joe Walsh.

FRANK: The trade unionist?

HELEN: That's right.

FRANK: You should have said so before. I was beginning to think you might be one of the other sort.

HELEN: (*Smiling*) I'm not. But Michael is.

(MICHAEL *looks extremely uncomfortable.*)

FRANK: Are you?

MICHAEL: Yes. I am.

FRANK: Well, I wouldn't worry about it, son. It's not being a Protestant what counts, it's being on the right side.

HELEN: What side is that, Mr Molloy?

FRANK: Don't call me Mr Molloy. Everybody calls me Frank. (*The door opens.* BRIDIE *appears with a tea tray and sandwiches.*) Bridie, do you know who this is? (BRIDIE *scrutinizes* HELEN.) This is Joe Walsh's wee girl.

BRIDIE: 'Course it is. You're the spittin' image of him.

FRANK: And this is Michael – what did you say your name was?

MICHAEL: Canning. Michael Canning.

(*She puts the tray down and hands the cups of tea around.*)

BRIDIE: (*To* HELEN) I was in the swimmers with your mammy once. That was when we were girls. Of course she's a good bit older than me. That was before I got married. I didn't swim after I met Frankie.

(*Laughter, shared by* HELEN.)

I haven't seen Rose for years. Is she well?

HELEN: She's very well.

BRIDIE: Well, tell her I was asking for her.

HELEN: I will.

BRIDIE: (*Withdrawing*) I'll put the pot back on the stove to keep it warm.

(*She closes the door.*)

HELEN: Is Colm one of the boys, though?

FRANK: No. That's his trouble. He doesn't know where to put himself.

HELEN: Well, if he's not, and you're sure he's not, then maybe we have a job for him.

MICHAEL: Helen!

HELEN: I need to do the interviews in Andersonstown with the women relatives. But we also need someone to interview the men. Fergus isn't going to have a lot of time with that book on punishment, and since Colm knows Andersonstown better than any of us, he might be just the person for the job. That's if he'd like to.

FRANK: Like to? He'd be delighted.

HELEN: We could also pay him.

MICHAEL: (*Groaning*) Helen!

FRANK: You know, he'd be very good.

HELEN: (*To* MICHAEL) It's perfect.

MICHAEL: You might be right, but you should really wait until you've spoken to Fergus.

HELEN: (*Firmly*) Bring Colm to the meeting on Monday.

16. INT. THE WALSHES' LIVING ROOM. FALLS ROAD. WEST BELFAST. EVENING. 9.00 PM.

JOE WALSH *is sitting at his work table in the bay window of the living room; he is finishing a piece of correspondence.* HELEN *is sitting on the sofa surrounded by her work for* FERGUS*: copies of law reports. She is reading the evening* Belfast Telegraph. JOE *gets up to look for a container for the paper he has been writing on. He can't resist looking at the papers around* HELEN. *He is curious about her work.* ROSE *is at the dining-room table with her seating arrangement for the wedding. Time: 9 April 1979.*

HELEN: (*Putting down the paper, to* JOE) Some group calling itself the Irish National Liberation Army has claimed responsibility for Neave's murder.

ROSE: (*To* JOE) The Sullivans can't come. That means we can ask Jim Quinn and Liam Brady.

HELEN: Irish National Liberation Army? Who are they?

JOE: They're a breakaway group from the Officials.

ROSE: Joe!

HELEN: The Official IRA are socialists. Are the INLA?

JOE: That crowd? The only socialism the INLA recognize is national socialism!

ROSE: Joe! Did you hear me? We can ask Jim Quinn and Liam Brady. The only trouble is they're widowers. (JOE *is looking blank.*) Could we put them on the same table or would that be too morbid? What do you think?

JOE: Put what on the same table?

ROSE: Jim Quinn and Liam Brady.

JOE: Rose, what are we talking about?

ROSE: Oh for God's sake, Joe. Would you ever listen to me. The wedding. Can we put Jim and Liam on the same table at the reception. Or would they just talk about their wives?

JOE: You know best, Rose. You do what you like.

ROSE: (*Hurt*) I was only asking. (*She gets up from the table and goes to the kitchen.*) I'm sorry to have interrupted your intellectual conversation.

JOE: (*Sighs. He sits down beside* HELEN.) Your mammy says you're working for Fergus Sloan. He's doing a book?

HELEN: On punishment. He's looking at the prison system. He's also writing a pamphlet on the H-Block protest. I'm supposed to be setting up the interviews in Andersonstown. I had to see Frank Molloy today. He sends his regards.

JOE: (*Stubbornly*) The Molloys are Provos.

HELEN: (*Shocked*) They're still people. Ordinary human beings like you and me. (*Quotes.*) 'I am human. I count nothing human alien to me.'

JOE: (*Gets up from beside her immediately.*) Oh Jesus. You've been away a long time. All we need is you to come back and tell us how to behave.

HELEN: (*Nervously*) I don't know what to say. You asked me what I was doing and I told you. You dismiss it. I defend it. What do you expect me to do?

JOE: I don't expect you to come back here and work for the Provos!

HELEN: Daddy, what's happening in the Maze affects everybody.

JOE: Fergus Sloan walks past me in the street.

HELEN: You always do this to me. You always confront me with loyalties. You or Fergus. You or Cliff. You or –

JOE: (*Furious, gets to his feet.*) Is that so?

HELEN: (*Quickly gets to her feet.*) Yes it is so!

JOE: I'm to blame for your marriage failure!

HELEN: I didn't say that. God Almighty, I wish you and my mother would stop using the word failure about me.

JOE: What word would you like me to use? Success?

HELEN: Look Daddy. I played it all the way along the line your way. I went to university. I did a law degree. I didn't go to art college.

JOE: You went to a university but sure you threw it all away when you went to work in the library. A librarian! What kind of satisfaction is that for anyone. Have you no responsibility for what you owe the people who fought for your right to an education? I don't see you coming to work for the Trade Unions! I don't see you giving the Labour Movement anything back.

(ROSE *comes out of the kitchen.*)

ROSE: For God's sake, are you two at it again? You know what's wrong with you, Joe, she's too like you.

JOE: If I'd had half her chances I'd have made something of myself by now. (*To* HELEN) I left school at eleven.

HELEN: You can't blame me for that!

JOE: And that was staying on longer than anybody else in the street because the parish priest persuaded my mother to send me back for another year to keep the attendance numbers up so that the schoolmaster could get his salary.

HELEN: It happened to you, not to me. It happened to you!

(*Focus on* HELEN*'s face.*)

JOE: You can't say that. Listen to me: my family came from the country to the city for work – from the wheat fields to the flour mills. I grew up as a barefoot boy in the Falls. I sold sticks – firewood – for money. From the orange-boxes that the greengrocer left in the entry. I didn't get my first pair of boots until I joined the Fianne. It was part of the uniform. I also got my first coat that way: a long green coat. And the Fianne ran the history classes at night. I was interned when I was seventeen and I read Kier Hardie in prison. When I came out I was a socialist. (JOE *turns away from her, and goes to his wife who is sitting nervously by the table. He sits, while he continues.*) You didn't have to join the IRA to get an education or boots or a coat – a Labour government in England saved you from that fate. A welfare state and a new Education Act. So you can't say it hasn't happened to you.

HELEN: (*Following him across the room*) When I first went into grammar school and I came home with a copy of *Macbeth* in my schoolbag, I was so excited I showed it to you. And you said: 'I read that in prison.' You've never let me forget what I owe. You want me to be somebody else. You always have. (*She is nearly in tears.*)

JOE: That's a damn lie! (*He gets to his feet again.*)

ROSE: Oh stop this, please. Everybody's fighting at the moment.

I'm sick of it. All I want is a quiet house.

(HELEN *walks away across the room.*)

JOE: Have you made your mind up whether you're going or staying here yet?

HELEN: Yes. I'm moving tomorrow. Michael's flat is empty while he's in Dublin on sabbatical. He wants me to keep an eye on the place for him.

JOE: Where's his flat?

HELEN: Stranmillis.

JOE: (*A last thrust*) Oh aye. I didn't expect it would be in the Falls.

(*She quickly picks up all her papers.*)

HELEN: I'll leave my phone number in case you want to ring me.

(*She goes to leave the room.*)

ROSE: You'll be coming to the wedding?

HELEN: I don't know. The last thing I feel like at the moment is a wedding.

(HELEN *leaves.* ROSE *turns to* JOE *bewildered.*)

17. INT. KELLY'S CELLARS. DAY. 2.30 PM.

Interior of Kelly's Cellars, a pub at the edge of West Belfast. Saturday, 12 May 1979. HELEN *and* COLM *are sitting at a table in the corner of a long bar. They have the interviews they have been collecting on the table in front of them.*

HELEN: (*Turning over the pages of her notes and reading*) Listen to this. Mrs Macken says she keeps washing her son's underclothing and sending them into the prison, but he never sends any out. She says she thinks he's too embarrassed.

COLM: (*Slowly*) How does she manage to wash them if he never sends any out?

HELEN: Well, that's what she says. And there's a girl here – she's seventeen – Kathleen Tolan, who got engaged six months ago to a nineteen year old who's on the blanket –

my God, Colm, he's the same age as you! She sees him once a month for a visit and he's in for twenty years. She says the Charismatic Movement has done wonders for her. (*Pause.*) How did your interviews with the men go?

COLM: I've written them up. You can read them yourself. (*He hands over his notes from the table.*) Do you want another drink?

HELEN: (*Scanning the notes without lifting her head*) No thanks. (*Pause.*) You know you write very well. Have you ever thought of it?

COLM: What's your interest?

HELEN: My interest?

COLM: Yes. What interest is it of yours whether I write or not?

HELEN: Oh Colm. Do you always have to be so prickly? It's like trying to get close to a hedgehog. I just wanted to help you.

COLM: What does helping me do for you? Solve your guilt about not living in Andersonstown?

HELEN: I don't have any guilt.

COLM: Oh, I think you do. And what's more, you think that if you can come back here and redeem one poor soul, throw a few encouraging phrases my way, you might just take the edge off it.

HELEN: You are foul. (*Slams the paper down on the table.*)

COLM: (*Slight pause.*) Actually I do write.

HELEN: You do? What do you write?

COLM: Poetry.

HELEN: Poetry?

COLM: Don't look so surprised. Andersonstown's full of poets.

HELEN: Will you show me your poems?

COLM: Aye. Some time. (*Pause.*) I haven't written anything for ages.

HELEN: Why?

(MONA *is standing over them holding a bundle of newspapers over her arm. They have not seen her arrive.*)

MONA: Hello, Colm.

COLM: Hello, Mona. Long time no see.

MONA: I hear you're too busy these days.

COLM: This is Mona O'Hare.

HELEN: Hello.
COLM: Do you know Helen Walsh?
MONA: I can't say that I do.
COLM: She grew up down the road from you. On the Falls.
MONA: So I hear. Do you still live there?
HELEN: No. But my parents do.
MONA: It's funny about you growing up on the Falls and yet nobody knows you.
HELEN: I don't make my friends on the basis of territory.
MONA: On what basis do you make your friends?
COLM: Mona, are you selling those papers?
MONA: I am. Ten pence or whatever you want to donate.
(*He hands her fifty pence.*)
COLM: Keep the change.
(MONA *leaves a newspaper on the table*)
MONA: Thanks. I'll be seeing you.
(HELEN *is watching her go. Focus on* HELEN*'s face.*)
HELEN: She was very aggressive.
COLM: She's not aggressive, she's intolerant, that's all. I think it's a very attractive quality.
HELEN: Well, it's not the most obviously attractive thing about her.
COLM: You know your trouble, Helen, you don't think politically.
HELEN: (*Laughs.*) Are you trying to tell me that when you look at Mona you see her politics. She has a beautiful face.
(*Hold on* COLM*'s face.*)
COLM: Jesus. You say she's beautiful but you can't see what it is that's beautiful about her; it's not her face, it's her commitment – it's so total and unrelenting. She doesn't look for approval from anyone, man or woman, in or out of uniform. She's incorruptible because she puts her politics first. That's what's beautiful about her. (*Pause.*) Anyway, she's got a sister in Armagh Gaol.
HELEN: Is she on the dirty protest?
COLM: Yes.
HELEN: Maybe I should talk to her.

COLM: I don't think Mona wants to talk about it.

HELEN: (*Extremely uncomfortable*) My sister's getting married today.

COLM: You didn't go to the wedding?

HELEN: I haven't been inside a church in years. Look, I'd quite like to go to the reception. (*She puts her hand on his arm.*) We could look in on the way to the flat.

COLM: Aye, all right.

(HELEN *smiles at him gratefully.*)

HELEN: You can act as buffer between me and my family. They won't shout at me if I have someone with me.

18. INT. RECEPTION ROOM. HOTEL GREENAN LODGE. DAY. 3.30 PM.

Interior of reception room at the Hotel Greenan Lodge. JOE WALSH *is standing up to make a speech at the top table. Background noises of glasses and tableware soften as he rises to his feet and raps on the table for silence.*

JOE: I'm not fond of making speeches, as you all know. (*Laughter and groans from the guests.*) So I'll make this as brief as possible. I'd like to give my blessing to my youngest daughter, Pauline – (*Focus on the smiling bride*) who today has married – (*He pauses to think of the name.*) Jim Johnson. When she came to tell me six months ago she said, 'Daddy, we'd like to get married.' You notice, it's the women in my family who do the talking. So I said to Jim, 'There's only one condition, if you want to marry a daughter of mine.' 'What's that?' Jim asked, rather nervously. 'That you're a member of a union – because if you're going to marry one of my girls – you'll need all the help you can get!' (*Laughter from the guests.*) Of course, with three daughters married now, Noreen and Vincent in Dublin, Helen and Cliff in England – (ROSE*'s jaw tightens.*) and now Pauline to Jim, I'm not so bossed as I used to be. All I can say is that I hope Pauline and Jim's union will be as successful as mine. With my wife that is. (*Laughter and applause.*) And now I'd like to propose a toast. (*He lifts his glass. Sound of chairs moving back and people rising.*) To the bride and groom. And may all their troubles – be little shop stewards! (*Laughter and chatter.*)

19. INT. RECEPTION ROOM. DAY.

HELEN *and* COLM *are by the door of the reception room. Cut from the wedding speech immediately to this shot. Use the laughter to link them.*

HELEN: I'll just see my sister and then we'll go.
ROSE: (*Coming towards them*) Helen!
(HELEN *looks at her mother's face, and turns to* COLM.)
HELEN: Oh God. If this looks like getting difficult, rescue me.
ROSE: (*Arriving at her side*) I'd like a word with you, please. (*She takes* HELEN *by the arm,* COLM *moves away, glass in hand.*) What are you doing here? You said you wouldn't be at the wedding!
HELEN: I changed my mind. I thought it would be nice to wish Pauline and Jim good luck.
ROSE: What do you mean turning up with that young man. Who is he?
HELEN: He's working with me. (*Pause.*) Look, I'll just say hello to Pauline and then I'll go.
ROSE: You're not going to say hello to anyone. You're leaving this minute and you're taking that young man with you. Honestly Helen. Turning up like this. What are my neighbours going to say, and you a married woman. Oh my God . . . (*She catches sight of* MRS MCCOY *who is approaching with a broad grin on her face.*) Don't turn round. There's Mrs McCoy. And she's the biggest gossip there is.
MRS MCCOY: Helen! (*They both turn and grin at her.*) I didn't know you were over.
HELEN: Hello, Sadie. Nice to see you.
(MRS MCCOY, *medium close up, as she turns to look away at*

PAULINE *who is still at the top table.*)

MRS MCCOY: Isn't Pauline looking lovely? Isn't her dress just lovely? (*She turns to* HELEN *again.*) Are you not sorry now you didn't get married in white?

HELEN: It's not my style.

MRS MCCOY: Is your husband not with you?

(ROSE*'s jaw tightens again. She is staying very close to* HELEN.)

HELEN: No. He's not.

MRS MCCOY: Oh?

HELEN: We're sep . . . (ROSE *tightens her grip on* HELEN*'s arm.*) we're having separate holidays.

MRS MCCOY: (*Looking at both mother and daughter*) Oh, very nice. Of course it's not very good weather for you, is it?

(COLM *arrives at* HELEN*'s other arm*)

COLM: Helen, are you ready to go yet?

HELEN: Ah Colm! Yes. I'm just leaving now. We have to go. Sorry, we're working today.

MRS MCCOY: (*Looking with interest at* COLM) What sort of work are you doing?

ROSE: She's writing a book.

HELEN: Mummy!

MRS MCCOY: Is she? What sort of book?

ROSE: (*Wildly*) It's called – Crime and Punishment.

(HELEN *raises her eyes.*)

HELEN: Mummy!

(COLM *grabs* HELEN *by the arm.*)

COLM: Come on Helen. I'm away.

(*They hurry away. The two women stare after them,* ROSE *looking worried and* MRS MCCOY *very interested.*)

MRS MCCOY: Isn't that Bridie Molloy's nephew!

(*They turn to face each other, eye to eye.*)

ROSE: Is it?

MRS MCCOY: Yes, I'm sure it is. I didn't think your Helen knew the Molloys.

ROSE: She doesn't. He's helping her, that's all.

20. INT. FERGUS'S ROOM. STRANMILLIS. DAY. 4.30 PM.

Fergus's room in Stranmillis. Late November 1979. FERGUS *is looking through Colm's interviews. He is sitting at his table.* HELEN *and* COLM *are standing watching a little way away.*

FERGUS: (*Looking up*) You did a fine job on these interviews, Colm. Did you keep the original notes?
HELEN: Those are his notes.
FERGUS: Well, you can certainly wield a pen. This will save me a lot of work.
COLM: If that's it then, I'll be on my way. (*He moves to the door.*)
HELEN: What about the book? The book. You were going to give him a copy of your book on terrorism.
(FERGUS *gets up. He moves to the bookcase; very untidy bookcase. He has several copies of his own book, neatly stacked.*)
FERGUS: Of course. Here we are. (*He moves to* COLM.) You can keep this copy, it's spare.
(*The title of the book is* Terrorism and the democratic ideal. COLM *holds it in his hand while he reads the title, then looks at* FERGUS.)
COLM: I won't keep it; I'll borrow it.
FERGUS: No. Please. It's the least I can do.
(HELEN *moves closer to the two men.*)
COLM: You don't owe me anything. I got paid for the interviews. (*Looks at* HELEN.)
FERGUS: Goodbye. (*He holds out his hand to* COLM.) Good luck.
(COLM *shakes hands with* FERGUS.)
COLM: And you. (*He is about to go. To* HELEN) I'll see you later.
(HELEN *nods.*)
FERGUS: I'll see you out.
COLM: I know the way.
(*He leaves them standing in the middle of the room.*)
FERGUS: You seem very taken by your protégé.
HELEN: He's not my protégé. Quite the reverse. (*Pause.*) So.

What happens now?

FERGUS: What happens now?

HELEN: To the H-Block protest.

FERGUS: Oh that. It goes to Strasbourg next month for admissibility.

HELEN: Admissibility?

FERGUS: Yes. A case can't go before the Commission until it's been passed by a Committee which decides if there is a case for taking it before the European Court in the first place.

HELEN: I see.

FERGUS: Everything has to have been tried to remedy the situation in the claimant's own country. It's a kind of court of last resorts.

(*He is trying to catch her eye, but she refuses to look directly at him.*)

HELEN: And what about the pamphlet, when will you write that?

FERGUS: My publisher's very keen. I'm hoping to bring it out early next year. But I'd like to know the result of the Strasbourg decision first. Helen – (*He catches her eye now.*) He's ten years younger than you.

HELEN: It's none of your business – any more.

FERGUS: Christ! You walk back into my life –

(*The door opens.* CASSANDRA *comes into the room carrying two bags full of groceries.*)

CASSANDRA: Oh I'm sorry, I didn't realize – (*She looks at* HELEN *and puts the shopping down.*) Helen Walsh!

HELEN: Yes. Cassandra McCullough.

CASSANDRA: (*To* FERGUS) So.

FERGUS: Helen is Michael's research assistant.

CASSANDRA: Michael's research assistant?

HELEN: Why didn't you tell her?

CASSANDRA: Is she involved in this H-Block business too? Oh, how like old times. Another star-struck protester living in a never-never land of protest marches and continuous revolution. (*She is walking around* HELEN *as she says this, looking at her youthfulness.*) Who does your supermarket shopping; your mother?

HELEN: (*Furious*) I do my own. I'd better go.

(*She walks out very quickly.*)

FERGUS: Helen! Wait a minute! (*She slams the door. Turning on* CASSANDRA) Christ, woman. I am tired of your jealousy.

CASSANDRA: (*Sits down, crushed.*) And I'm tired too, Fergus. Very tired. I'm tired defending something I don't believe in any more.

FERGUS: Something or someone?

CASSANDRA: I met Sally Stewart in the supermarket. You do remember our great friends the Stewarts? They were at our wedding. We went on holiday with them. And in Donegal when Sally and I got drunk together she held my head while I puked. Actually she held my hair up out of the vomit, while you walked away and would have nothing to do with us.

FERGUS: I remember the Stewarts. What's all this in aid of?

CASSANDRA: She walked straight past me. So I went after her. 'Sally, what's wrong?' I said. 'I see Fergus is still writing to the newspapers,' she said. 'Ask him from me, will you, if that prison officer who was shot dead last night had any human rights at all?' (*Pause.*) Fergus! Well?

FERGUS: What do you expect from me?

CASSANDRA: I don't expect you to defend murderers.

FERGUS: Everything I do now you're against. There's not one thing about me you admire or support any more. Not one.

CASSANDRA: Your causes are destroying us!

21. EXT. BELFAST CITY CENTRE. NIGHT.

December 1979. Belfast city centre after eleven o'clock. HELEN *and* COLM *are walking towards the security gates in Castle Street from the town centre side of the gates going towards the Falls Road. They have been drinking at Kelly's Cellars. She has her arm through his.*

HELEN: Fergus says the cases are through. They've passed Admissibility. They go to the European Court now.

COLM: When?
HELEN: The hearing has been set for next March.
COLM: Three months. When will they reach a decision?
HELEN: That I don't know.
(COLM *stops. They have reached the gates.*)
COLM: Shit! (*He moves away from her arm.*)
HELEN: What is it?
COLM: They're locked.
(*He is staring solemnly ahead of him at the locked gates and at the Falls Road beyond.* HELEN *reaches out her hand to touch him.*)
HELEN: We can go the other way.
COLM: Agh. This town depresses me! (*Moving in to grip the bars of the gates with both hands*) They're driving us back all the time. Back into the ghetto.
(*Hold on his hands on the gates.*)

22. EXT. NIGHT.

Dream. Black and white. Same location as scene 21. HELEN *is alone on a dark road: in reality, this is Castle Street, the edge of the town. She turns to find she is being followed by four uniformed shadowy figures in black; she breaks into a run, but no matter how hard she runs they are always the same distance away. Suddenly, she breaks away from her pursuers and runs towards the security gates. They are locked. Sobbing, she grips the gates with her hands, as if to shake them apart. Through the gate she can see* COLM *in profile. He does not respond to her. He seems unable to see or hear her. Still crying and with all her force she continues to grip and shake the gates – but is unable to open them. Her terror and an atmosphere of trapped inevitability is essential.*

23. INT. MOLLOYS' HOUSE. NIGHT.

HELEN *wakes up trembling and sobbing. She and* COLM *are asleep in a single bed by the wall in the Molloys' house in Andersonstown. He has his arm around her.*

COLM: Shush, shush, Helen. What is it?

HELEN: (*Opening her eyes*) I was having a nightmare.

COLM: I know. The whole bed shook.

HELEN: (*Speaking very rapidly*) I was alone on a dark road trying to get to somewhere –

COLM: Shush. You'll waken Bridie.

HELEN: Behind me I could see shadows, men in black in some kind of uniform –

COLM: Easy. Easy.

HELEN: And they were following me. I couldn't get through and I couldn't go back!

COLM: It's only a dream, love. Don't upset yourself. I have those dreams too.

HELEN: Hold me. Oh God! Colm, I'm so frightened.

COLM: You'll be all right, love.

BRIDIE: (*Voice over*) Colm! Colm!

COLM: Oh Jesus Christ! It's Bridie!

BRIDIE: Colm! (*Opening the bedroom door*) Get up quick, the Army and the police are outside. (*She is now in the room.*) Colm! (*She can suddenly see both of them.*) In the name a'Jesus! I said she could stay here. I didn't say she could sleep in your bed!

COLM: What is it? What's wrong?

(*The room is tiny. The window, which has venetian blinds, is at the foot of the bed.* BRIDIE *moves towards it.*)

BRIDIE: It's a raid. (*Turns.*) I think they're going to raid us. They're all over the road, and they're at the back of the house. I've been watching them from the window.

COLM: What time is it?

BRIDIE: Five o'clock. Get up quick, Helen. Get you into the spare bed immediately. (*Sound of door hammering. She moves quickly to the bedroom door.*) Ah Holy God, that's it. It's started. (*The bed creaks.* HELEN *pushes back the bedclothes to get up.* BRIDIE *turns her head.*) Oh Jesus, Mary and Joseph! (*She watches* HELEN *who is climbing out of bed over* COLM *in the dark.*) Have you no nightdress on! Oh my God! Oh Holy God! (*Front door hammering continues.*) Cover yourself up!

(*She grabs a blanket off the bed and pushes it at* HELEN.) In the name a' Jesus! Oh Holy God, this is a punishment. (*To* COLM) I knew the minute I said she could stay this would happen. Now it'll be all over the estate. (COLM*'s face is totally unresponsive.*) Your mammy'll kill me, Helen Walsh. (HELEN *gazes at her unrepentant.*) And it's just as well your Uncle Frank's on night work, my lad! I don't know what he'd say. (*Front door hammering again*) I'm coming, I'm coming. Hold your horses!

(*She leaves.* HELEN *is standing in the blanket by the bed. Cut on* HELEN *standing with the blanket round her shoulders. Her stance should resemble the photo of the blanket women in the magazine she looked at at the beginning of the play.*)

24. INT. MOLLOYS' LIVING ROOM. NIGHT. 10.50 PM.

The evening after the raid. HELEN *has a basin of water by her on the table. She is standing over* COLM *who is sitting in an upright chair. She is wiping a wound on his head with a cloth. She rinses it out in the basin and hands it back to* COLM.

HELEN: Here, put this on it. (COLM, *his eyes very bruised as well, takes the damp cloth, reacts in pain as he puts it to his face.*) That eye looks awful.

COLM: (*Holding the cloth to his eye*) Never mind that. Who got me out?

HELEN: (*Drying her hands on the towel she has placed on the table by the basin*) Fergus. I asked him to. I told him about your brother and the bank robberies. And that he'd skipped off to Belgium so you'd been picked up instead. He drove me straight to Castlereagh. I was really scared, Colm.

COLM: He's a good man is Fergus.

HELEN: I know. I felt sorry for him. He seemed very alone and buried in his work. He told me Cassandra had left him –

COLM: (*Extremely irritated*) It's a pity he's such a fool. (*Takes the cloth from his eye.*) Here, take this thing away.

HELEN: (*Takes the cloth.*) Why is he a fool?

COLM: Because he's so sincere. He's like you. There's a war on and you're still playing the game by the rules.

HELEN: He helped you. Why is he a fool?

COLM: It just seems a pity to disappoint him.

HELEN: Disappoint him?

COLM: I'm going to Dublin tonight.

HELEN: (*Carefully*) Are we?

COLM: No. I am.

HELEN: But you can't. You're on bail. Fergus put up two hundred pounds for you.

COLM: (*Gets up.*) Well, if his book's a best seller he can recoup his losses.

HELEN: I don't understand any of this.

COLM: He's got something out of the troubles too, you know. He wouldn't have been able to write *Terrorism and the Democratic Ideal*, if it wasn't for us.
(*He stoops swiftly to the coffee table and picks the book up.*)

HELEN: (*Bewildered*) For us?

COLM: (*Hands her the book.*) Yes. You can give him his book back now. (*She refuses to take it. He puts it down again. Quotes without opening the book.*) 'That although the IRA is fanatical we have to recognize the democratic principle – their right to a fair trial – the rule of law and all the apparatus of the legal process – because, if not, the liberal democrat is transformed by the suspension of the democratic principle – in itself an act of violence – is transformed so that he ceases to be a liberal and becomes in turn a fanatic.' He's a great thinker, is Fergus. Unfortunately that is all he can do.

HELEN: You seem to have got that word perfect.

COLM: I have a talent for remembering.

HELEN: Colm, I know you're angry. But if you jump bail that's tantamount to a confession.

COLM: That's right.

HELEN: You told me you weren't mixed up with the Provos.

COLM: I'm not.
HELEN: Then why?
COLM: Irish National Liberation Army.
HELEN: (*Devastated*) Since when?
COLM: Does it matter?
HELEN: Oh God. What have I done!
COLM: I was ten when the troubles started. My uncle took me with him on that demonstration to Derry. I didn't even know what it was about. I just remember the police baton-charging us – and the men running and the screams. I remember my Uncle Frank lying on the road with blood on his face. I don't know why, but I knew then I was in.
HELEN: (*Weakly*) You mean you did the bank jobs?
COLM: The less you know the better. (*Checks his watch. It is five to eleven.*) I'm crossing the border in two and a half hours. One of the boys will be calling in a minute.
HELEN: How do they know you're out?
COLM: Everybody in the road knows I've been released.
HELEN: But you're a poet. Doesn't that mean anything? You have a voice. An alternative to this.
COLM: Padric Pearse and Joseph Mary Plunkett were poets; and James Connolly's prose is beautiful.
HELEN: Of course. How could I forget. (*Pause.*) I thought once, we were together.
COLM: You women are all alike! There's a war on and all you think of is being together, happy families, making cups of tea. You're as bad as Bridie; she'd make tea for the troops if you'd let her.
HELEN: What will I do now? I can't stay here. (*She sits.*)
COLM: You'll never be stuck Helen. You'll find some trendy English intellectual with a taste for adventure, an Irish ancestor and a guilt complex as big as your own, and he'll take care of you. (HELEN *turns her face away in distress.*) And when you're happily settled in your house on Hampstead Heath you can always tell your grandchildren that you knew me.
HELEN: (*Facing him again*) I passed that point before. I'm

talking about now.

COLM: Well, you could always try Fergus!

HELEN: Agh! (*Closes her eyes.*) *Mea culpa, mea culpa, mea maxima culpa.*

COLM: (*Furious*) What did you say that for?

HELEN: It was a response I once learned. (*Pause.*) You sound as though you hate me.

COLM: I don't hate you. I don't have any time for women like you, that's all. (*A very soft knock on the window is heard, then repeated. For a moment* COLM *looks worried.*) That may be the signal. You'd better answer it, just in case. (HELEN *goes to the living room door.* COLM *picks up the basin and towel and quickly exits to the kitchen.* HELEN *comes back into the room followed by* MONA. COLM *re-enters from the kitchen and goes immediately to* MONA.)

If we're stopped we're a courting couple.

HELEN: (*Bitterly*) You use love as a disguise!

COLM: (*Stung*) Love! Oh, that's just typical of the level of your response.

HELEN: (*Broken*) But only two nights ago you –

(*He is frozen with fear and rage.*)

MONA: Oh come on, we've nothing against her. (*She grabs his arm.*) Don't make it worse.

COLM: Goodbye Helen. Don't forget to give Fergus his book – tell him I enjoyed the lesson.

(*She looks down at the cloth she has been holding to dress his wound.*)

25. EXT. BELFAST. 10.00 AM.

Belfast. End of May 1980.

FERGUS *comes out of Queen's bookshop with a paper bag of books under his arm. He walks diagonally towards the corner of the street facing Queen's University old building.* TWO JOGGERS, *a man and a woman, pass. As he watches them,* JOE WALSH *appears. The two men have not met or spoken for many years: they regard each other in silence. Another* JOGGER *passes. Then* JOE *gives way first and nods at* FERGUS. *He goes on towards the bookshop.* FERGUS *hesitates, then turns back and goes after* JOE.

26. INT. UPSTAIRS DRAWING ROOM OF A LARGE HOUSE IN HOLLAND PARK. DAY. 1.00 PM.

June 1980. London. A wedding party is in progress. All of the guests have gone downstairs to the buffet in the dining room. FERGUS *and* MICHAEL *are sitting on two upright chairs at the far end of the room by the window. The windows – early Georgian – are full-length and the ceiling very high in contrast to the Andersonstown interiors. There are empty and half-full glasses of wine around the room on different tables and at the foot of some chairs, also empty Champagne bottles. There is a half-full bottle resting on the table by* MICHAEL. *The whole effect is of a wealthy colonial drawing room.* FERGUS*'s opening words can be voiced over and through a camera perusal of the surroundings: Renaissance paintings and Turkish carpets. There are occasional sounds of guests talking and dishes from downstairs.*

FERGUS: The European Court entirely agreed with the British authorities on Political Prisoner status. The case against the Republicans was that they haven't identified any beliefs such as agnosticism or pacifism. Belief is the key word in Article 9.

(MICHAEL *is holding a copy of the Strasbourg Report and looking at it while* FERGUS *is talking.*)

MICHAEL: Article 9?

FERGUS: The Declaration of Human Rights. (*Quotes.*) Everyone has the right to freedom of thought, conscience and religion; this includes freedom to change his religion or belief –

MICHAEL: (*Nodding*) Of course. How could I forget. You sat up all night before we occupied Stormont on Human Rights Day in 'sixty-nine and learned it!

FERGUS: (*Smiling at the memory*) Anyway, the British authorities argued that 'belief' in Article 9 relates to the holding of a philosophical or spiritual conviction which has to have an identifiable formal content – it doesn't extend to deeply held feeling which they call 'opinions'.

MICHAEL: And Political Prisoner status – Special Category status is deemed an 'opinion' not a 'belief'?

FERGUS: Exactly. So the authorities won. The European Court threw the case out. And the situation in Long Kesh is much as before. I'll have to put an appendix in the book explaining the Commission's report. I don't care what anyone says; terrorism and housebreaking are not the same!

MICHAEL: What will happen now?

FERGUS: It's being published in September.

MICHAEL: I mean the situation in the Maze.

FERGUS: The Republicans have threatened a hunger strike. (MICHAEL *looks in disbelief.*) Well, they threatened it before with Whitelaw over the same issue.

MICHAEL: I don't think the British would want that, do you? (CASSANDRA *comes into the room from the side, looking for them.*)

CASSANDRA: Oh come on, you two. Stop talking shop! It's Michael's wedding day!

MICHAEL: You're quite right. Kate would kill me for this. Have you spoken to her yet?

CASSANDRA: I can't get near her. She's surrounded by photographers.

MICHAEL: (*Sighs.*) She usually is.

CASSANDRA: It's a beautiful house, Michael.

MICHAEL: Yes. It belongs to Kate's mother. The father was a tea planter.

CASSANDRA: Oh. (*She looks at* FERGUS.) Are you coming down to eat yet?

FERGUS: In a minute.

CASSANDRA: Can I get you something?

FERGUS: I'll be down in a minute. (*She goes off.* FERGUS *lifts his briefcase off the floor, opens it and puts the report away. He puts the case on the chair as he gets up from it.*) By the way, I bumped into Joe Walsh in Queen's bookshop a while ago.

He spoke to me for the first time in years.

MICHAEL: Did you ask about Helen?

FERGUS: (*Nodding*) He said he hasn't heard from her. She just went off without a word to anyone.

MICHAEL: No idea where she is?

FERGUS: Somewhere in England. That was all he said.

MICHAEL: I sent an invitation to her old address just on the off-chance that it might be forwarded. But it came back.

FERGUS: Yes. It was a pretty bad business.

MICHAEL: He's dead, you know. Shot by Loyalists.

FERGUS: So I heard. We'd better go and eat before Cassandra comes up again.

MICHAEL: Is everything working out there? (FERGUS *gives him a warning look.* MICHAEL *puts his hands up.*) All right, I'm sorry. It's none of my business.

(*They move away, leaving the briefcase on the chair. Cut on this shot.*)

27. EXT. BELFAST. ROSE AND JOE WALSH'S BACKYARD. MORNING. 10.40 AM.

18 December 1980. ROSE *has just come out of the door to put her rubbish into the bin. It is full. She slams the lid down and opens the top of a large plastic bag by the bin and forces the new bag of rubbish into the top. She looks around at the scattered bags of rubbish and sighs.*

ROSE: (*Calling*) Joe! Joe! Come out here till you see this. (JOE *comes out. He looks worried.*)

JOE: Rose, what is it? What's wrong.

ROSE: Look at this place! Look at the mess. It's been three weeks since my bins were lifted. And these plastic bags are useless. The cats have them pulled all over the yard.

JOE: (*Looks relieved.*) For God's sake, Rose, I thought there was something wrong. I told you it's a go-slow. Until the corporation stop cutting back on the men there'll be a go-slow. And I'm the one who's telling them to go slow. So there's no point in blaming the men. Go and protest to the Corporation.

ROSE: That's all very well, but what am I supposed to do with Christmas a week away? (*The back gate or door opens. They both turn quickly.*) In the name of God!

(HELEN *is standing with an artist's portfolio in one hand and a small rucksack in the other. She is greatly changed, principally thinner, even younger-looking, with the sucked-in face of someone who is travelling very fast. She has cut off her long hair, looking more like a boy.*)

HELEN: Hello Rose, Joe.

ROSE: What have you done to your hair? You look like something from Belsen!

JOE: I must admit I've seen better looking come out of the Maze myself.

28. INT. WALSHES' LIVING ROOM. MORNING. CONTINUOUS TIME.

ROSE: Noreen said she'd heard from you. I thought you would spend Christmas in Dublin.

HELEN: Sandycove was a bit too quiet for me.

ROSE: That's truer than you think. (*Pause.*) We could have had a lovely Christmas with Noreen and Vinny this year. But your father! I couldn't get him out of Belfast. And listen. I don't know what your university friends are up to, but I don't want you getting involved in this business. We're not supporting the hunger strike in this house.

HELEN: But you don't want them to die?

ROSE: I don't want anyone to die. I never did. But your father doesn't support those fellows. And the government shouldn't give in to them. Other people feel like us. Gerry Fitt stood up in the House of Commons and said it.

HELEN: Well, if you don't want them to die, we're on the same side.

ROSE: They're convicted criminals, murderers. You seem to

forget that. They aren't interned. They've all been through the courts.

HELEN: (*Patiently but stubbornly*) Some of those men in the Maze are there as a result of statements they signed during interrogation – statements which were used to convict them in court.

ROSE: (*Provoked to fury*) They're known terrorists, Helen! After all you've been through have you learned nothing about what liars they are!

HELEN: That has nothing to do with this argument. I was simply pointing out –

ROSE: I know what you're pointing out. I may not have a degree, but I'm not stupid. You and your university friends are all the same. Support the Hunger Strikers – but none of you live on the Falls Road! (HELEN *gives her mother a despairing look.*) You live in England and that's another world!

HELEN: (*Finally managing to speak*) Just once it would be nice to find that there was something about me that you approved of, Mummy.

ROSE: (*Stung*) Approve? How can I? Look at you! (*Cut to a single shot of* HELEN. ROSE *sits down, upset.*) You have no idea what we have to live through here. Nobody has. There are bin lids going at four in the morning, and knee-cappings, and hijackings; but not in the Protestant areas – oh no, here in West Belfast. (*Begins to weep.*)

HELEN: Please don't cry.

(JOE *comes into the room from upstairs.*)

JOE: I'm away on down town. Och, for goodness' sake. She's hardly in the house again and you're crying over her.

ROSE: (*Looks up at* JOE.) I was just telling her to keep her opinions to herself while she's here. We don't want her stabbing us in the back as well.

HELEN: What?

JOE: They've threatened to burn the homes of anyone who doesn't support the Hunger Strikers if any of them die. They're on the fifty-third day now and the last report said that Sean

McKenna is 'deteriorating rapidly'. So they've been round here these past couple of nights with their bin lids.

HELEN: Who has?

ROSE: Those women and girls. That one Mona's among them. He married her, you know.

(*Cut to Helen's reaction.*)

JOE: (*Looks quickly at* ROSE.) That's why we didn't go to Dublin for Christmas. It would have looked like we were running away.

HELEN: But why do they come here? You're not their enemy!

JOE: I'm not exactly on their side. You know my politics: bread-and-butter issues move me. I've never been all that interested in tribes. Look, I must go. This meeting's at eleven. See you later.

ROSE: (*Picking up*) I hope it's good news, Joe. I'm not going to give those boys a Christmas box if my bins aren't out of the backyard and emptied before Christmas. And you can tell them that.

(JOE *comes back from the door.*)

JOE: What do you mean you're not going to give them a Christmas box? I'm the one who has to pay for – (*He thinks better of it. Waves his hand as if to wipe the issue away. To* HELEN) Agh! Your mother's always the same. She sees only the effects of things on her. I'm away before we get into an argument.

(*He slams the door after him.* ROSE *gets up cheerfully now.*)

ROSE: Have you done your Christmas shopping yet? We could maybe go down town.

HELEN: Do you mind if we leave that until tomorrow?

(ROSE, *struggling with disappointment, but watching as* HELEN *picks up her portfolio.*)

ROSE: No. No. Have you something else to do today?

HELEN: I've got to go to Stranmillis.

ROSE: (*Angry*) Oh yes! Fergus Sloan!

HELEN: I'm not going to see anybody like that. If you must know, I'm going to see someone about getting some paintings exhibited.

ROSE: (*Suspicious*) Whose paintings?

HELEN: (*Reluctantly*) Mine. I've done some prints and sketches, which some people in England think are quite good. I'm at art college now.

ROSE: Why didn't you say so before? Your daddy'd be so proud of you.

HELEN: He would not. He'd probably say, 'Sure, I used to paint in gaol.'

(*Cut on Helen's expression.*)

29. EXT. STRANMILLIS ROAD. DAY. 2.30 PM.

HELEN *is passing the greystone church at the entrance to the quiet cul-de-sac where* FERGUS *lives. She looks wistfully towards the house, but goes on. Three joggers pass, running citywards.*

30. EXT. STRANMILLIS ROAD. DAY. CONTINUOUS TIME.

HELEN *is walking through the gates of the Arts Council building on the same road. Close on designation.*

31. INT. LIVING ROOM OF MOLLOYS' HOUSE. DAY.

HELEN *is sitting on the sofa with her portfolio beside her.* BRIDIE *is also sitting on the sofa.* FRANK *is sitting across by the fire, the wood carvings still in place. A white candle is burning in the window.*

FRANK: Are you over for long?

HELEN: Just for Christmas.

BRIDIE: You look like a wee young girl. (*Pause.*)

HELEN: Thank you.

BRIDIE: Are you at your mammy's?

HELEN: I am. Yes.

FRANK: So what are you doing with yourself these days?

HELEN: I'm painting.

FRANK: House painting?

HELEN: No, silk screen.

FRANK: Sounds very grand.

BRIDIE: Is that what you've got in the folder?

(HELEN *gets up to open the folder.*)

HELEN: Yes. Would you like to have a look?

(BRIDIE *and* FRANK *exchange glances.*)

BRIDIE: Oh – yes.

(HELEN *takes out a large silk-screen print in pastel colours of a room with two windows of different sizes with the blinds down and the light showing the frame of the window through the blinds.*)

FRANK: (*Sincerely*) What is it?

HELEN: What does it look like to you?

BRIDIE: Well, I'd say it was a picture of an empty room with the sunlight coming through the blinds.

FRANK: But why is the room empty?

HELEN: (*Close up on her face*) Because that is how it is.

(HELEN *puts the picture away in the folder.*)

BRIDIE: Well, I'm very glad you've found something, Helen. You were always a bit of a square peg in a round hole.

FRANK: Do you get paid for that?

HELEN: Not directly. (*She sits down again.*) But they are going to be exhibited in a gallery in town. And I will get paid if somebody buys them. (*She looks very uncomfortable.*) Look. I read about Colm in the paper. I'm very sorry. They said it was a Loyalist shooting.

FRANK: Don't kid yourself. That was the SAS.

HELEN: (*To* BRIDIE) And Brendan's on the Hunger Strike?

FRANK: Aye, he just joined it.

BRIDIE: Ah sure don't talk to me. I'll tell you something, Frank Molloy. If it comes to it, I won't let him die.

FRANK: (*Getting up*) What right have you to go interfering?

BRIDIE: He's my son. (*To* HELEN) Father Oliver says that a hunger striker's death is the worst thing you could listen to. He knew the priest at Wakefield Prison when that fellow Stagg died. The screams are terrible. It's the pains in the head, you see.

HELEN: (*Building up to this*) Bridie. (*Pause.*) Why are my parents being harassed?

BRIDIE: They're not being harassed. Who told you that?

HELEN: Joe says that some of the women come round at night with bin lids –

FRANK: Joe Walsh is sitting in that City Hall, a councillor, and he's said nothing about the H-Blocks.

(FRANK *is standing with his back to the fire.*)

BRIDIE: What do you expect, Helen? Some of those women have daughters in Armagh Gaol.

(FRANK *folds his arms across his chest.*)

FRANK: He spends far too much time talking to Loyalists, if you ask me.

HELEN: Maybe he thinks that you won't solve anything by bombing the Protestant working class into the Lough!

FRANK: (*Leaning forward*) Nobody's talking about bombing them into the Lough. We have to bomb them to the conference table.

HELEN: (*Wearily*) And how are they supposed to know the difference? (*Pause.*) Frank, my father is a trade unionist. If you drive him off the Falls – it will be like driving Connolly or Larkin away.

FRANK: He's no James Connolly. He's sold out to the Brits and the Unionists.

HELEN: And what about the Brits who are trade unionists?

FRANK: (*Pause.*) Nobody wants him to go off the Falls. If he goes out of the Falls it's his own look out!

HELEN: Get the Republicans to call the women off the house.

FRANK: Are you kidding? Those are mothers and daughters. Do you think we have any control over them?

HELEN: I once helped your nephew.

FRANK: I know that. And I'm very grateful. But this is frustration. It's only frustration. It'll come to nothing. Joe will just have to put up with it.

HELEN: I'd better be getting back.

(*She gets up to go.* BRIDIE *gets up with* HELEN.)

BRIDIE: Come on, I'll walk you down.

(*To* FRANK) I won't be long.

FRANK: (*Sensing something*) You're supposed to be going to the prison with me to see Brendan.

BRIDIE: Aye. But I've to go to Confession first.

32. EXT. ANDERSONSTOWN. SHAWS ROAD. NIGHT. 6.00 PM.

It is early evening, but dark and raining. HELEN *and* BRIDIE *are passing a supermarket, where* HELEN *can see about thirty people assembled.*
The murmur of their voices becomes clearer as she and BRIDIE *approach.*

BRIDIE: You know, everyone has their troubles these days.
(*They are passing the crowd, who are saying the rosary in Gaelic. All are holding rosary beads. One man at the centre is leading, the other voices respond.*)
It's not only your mammy and daddy.
(BRIDIE *doesn't even turn her head.* HELEN *never takes her eyes off the ceremony.*)

SINGLE VOICE: (*In Gaelic*)
Hail Mary, full of grace
The Lord is with thee.
Blessed art thou among women,
And blessed is the fruit of thy womb.

CHORUS: (*Rapidly in Gaelic*)
Holy Mary, Mother of God,
Pray for us sinners now,
And at the hour of our death. Amen.

HELEN: Bridie! What are those people doing there?

BRIDIE: They're saying the rosary.

HELEN: (*Nodding*) I can see that. But why?

BRIDIE: They gather there every night to pray for an end to the Hunger Strike.
(*Continue the murmur of the prayers. Hold on a long shot of the crowd with* HELEN *and* BRIDIE *in the foreground, walking away.*)

33. INT. LIVING ROOM. NIGHT.

Living room of Rose and Joe's house. The clamour of bin lids has brought ROSE *to the window. She puts the heavy curtain back to look out.*

ROSE: Oh Mother of God! They're here, Joe. They're here. Oh Mother of God.

JOE: Come away from that window! (*He pulls her away quickly.*) Get the back door closed.

(*He goes to the window himself and pulls the curtain back.* ROSE *turns towards the kitchen.*)

34. EXT. NIGHT.

A through-the-window shot of the torchlight demonstration. MONA *is clearly visible at the front.*)

JOE: (*Voice over*) Aye, they're out there all right.

35. INT. THE LIVING ROOM. NIGHT.

JOE *is at the window watching.* ROSE, *still turning towards the kitchen when the back door slams.*

ROSE: Oh Christ Almighty. It's too late, they're at the back as well.

JOE: (*Turns round quickly*) Jesus Christ, I told you –

(*They both stare in horror at the kitchen entrance when suddenly it is* HELEN *who arrives in the room followed by* BRIDIE.)

HELEN: It's all right, it's me. I've locked the door. (*Obvious relief on both their faces. Still breathless*) We saw the torches from the top of the street. There's a crowd of about thirty at the front. The word is that Sean McKenna's dying. (*Turns to* BRIDIE *who is standing behind her.*) Oh, this is Bridie Molloy.

ROSE: (*Nodding*) Yes. We know each other. (*To* JOE) Did you hear that, Joe? Sean McKenna's dying!

HELEN: Christ! What are the British trying to do to us?

JOE: It's not the British. The Secretary of State offered them concessions on December the fourth if they'd give up their hunger strike.

HELEN: What concessions?

JOE: He told them they could wear their own clothes for recreation and civilian clothing issued by the prison authorities during the normal working day.

HELEN: And Special Category status?

JOE: No. They didn't get that. They'll never get that. The concessions were made to all prisoners everywhere in Northern Ireland; it's a prison reform. There's no point in them dying now. They're dying because these people won't let them live. And that wee bitch Mona's out there, stirring them up.

HELEN: Mona?

JOE: I've just seen her.

HELEN: Bridie, you've got to stop them.

BRIDIE: If I couldn't stop my own son going on hunger strike, I can't stop that crowd putting you out of here.

HELEN: I'm going to try to talk to her.

JOE: Hold on, Helen, I'm coming with you. You stay here, Rose.

ROSE: Don't worry about me. I've no intention of going out of here tonight. They'll have to burn this house down round me.

36. EXT. OUTSIDE WALSHES' FRONT DOOR. NIGHT.

The noise in the street is terrifying, bin lids, chanting, and the torches burning.

VOICES: Brit lovers out. Out! Out! Out!

(HELEN *and her* FATHER *are standing at the front door, helpless before the sight confronting them. A long shot over and through the torch lights.* MONA *is standing in front of the demonstrators.*)

HELEN: Mona! Stop this! Get them to stop. (HELEN *moves towards the garden gate.*) Mona! (MONA *raises her hand and the bin lids stop. She approaches* HELEN *slowly.*) What are you doing here? This is where my father and mother live. (MONA *stands and watches her.*) Mona. You know me. Answer me! What are you trying to do?

MONA: I don't know you. Nobody knows you around here. Nobody's ever heard of you.

HELEN: Don't play stupid games with me, Mona! Of course you know me. I was a friend of Colm's. (MONA *moves in closer. The rest of the demonstrators remain farther away.*)

MONA: Colm's dead. He was murdered by the Brits. He's dead because of the likes of Joe Walsh – (JOE *is standing by the front door. He moves forward to the gate.*) who give tacit support to a corrupt regime by co-operating with it.

JOE: Is that what I do?

MONA: Yes. And we want you out of this house as a warning to the other Brit lovers. We want you off that council because you don't represent anybody here.

JOE: You'll not intimidate me off the council. And my wife says she'll not come out of there tonight. So what will you do? Not set fire to it. It wouldn't be very practical. They'd all go up. The whole row. And some of your friends there – (*Points to the crowd.*) live at the end of the block.

MONA: Oh, you think you're smart, Joe Walsh – but you're finished.

HELEN: Mona, why are you doing this? We live in the same kind of house as you. The same kind of street. My father and mother are part of the oppressed people it's supposed to be about. And yet you want to put them out? What makes you imagine that anyone would willingly support a government run by you, when you stoop to these methods? If you use force to get your support, you'll always have to use force to keep it.

MONA: Sean McKenna was moved to Musgrave Park Hospital. He's on the danger list. He'll die any minute. Pauline

McLoughlin in Armagh weighs four and a half stone; whether she dies or not is immaterial, she has probably damaged her womb, kidneys and liver – permanently. Some of us have been driven too far. Some of us are past talking! (*She turns and walks away. The bin lids start clamouring again.*)

VOICES: Out. Out. Out! Joe Walsh out. Brit lovers out.

JOE: (*Close up*) You can't reason with her. She's a vicious wee bitch.

HELEN: What do you think they'll do?

JOE: (*Watching the crowd in the middle of the road*) I don't know. But if that fellow dies tonight we've had it here.

VOICES: Out. Out. Out. Out. Out. Out. Out.

HELEN: I don't suppose we could get help from anywhere. I mean, call the police.

JOE: Are you kidding? It wouldn't be just a wrecked house we'd have on our hands. I wouldn't be responsible for bringing the police in here tonight.

VOICES: Brit lovers out. *Out. Out. Out.* Brit lovers out . . .

37. INT. LIVING ROOM. NIGHT.

Inside the living room. BRIDIE *and* ROSE *are sitting. Muffled chanting from the street.*

BRIDIE: I go to the prison most nights.

ROSE: Yes. I heard the others had joined in as well. I'm sorry for you, Bridie. It seems such a waste of life. (*Pause.*) God, who would have kids!

BRIDIE: Aye, they're a trouble.

ROSE: You sacrifice everything for them, and they throw it back in your face. That Helen one I just don't understand what she's got against us.

BRIDIE: Och now, she's very like you.

ROSE: She is not. She's not a bit like me. She's very like Joe.

BRIDIE: Oh she is. It's you she's like. She's very stubborn.

ROSE: Is your Brendan younger or older than Helen?

BRIDIE: Younger. We bought Helen's pram from you when I had Brendan. Do you not remember?

ROSE: Did you? Helen's pram? The big high one with the mother-of-pearl inlay and the canopy?

BRIDIE: That's right. It was a beautiful pram.

ROSE: Do you know something? I'd forgotten all about that.

(HELEN *bursts into the living room.*)

HELEN: Bridie. Come and talk to Mona. You're Colm's aunt – if you could get them to go home it might – it's our only chance.

BRIDIE: I'll talk to her but I don't think it'll do any good. I know Mona, she's very young. She's been a lot worse since Colm's murder. (*Gets up from the chair.*) Rose. (*Pause.*) If Sean McKenna dies, I can't be responsible for those women out there. You may have to walk out of here tonight.

ROSE: I'm not running this time.

BRIDIE: It isn't running. It's just being sensible, until things quieten down a bit.

ROSE: On the fourteenth of August 1969 we were burned out of Conway Street by Protestants. Joe was on night work at the flour mill –

HELEN: Mummy, don't!

ROSE: No, I'm going to tell it. There was only me and the girls at home. My husband stood on the roof of the mill with the other men and watched his home burning, and could do nothing! We had to run for our lives. We lost everything that night. Everything we ever owned. And we spent two years living like refugees until we were rehoused, and we came here. (*She begins to break down.*)

HELEN: Oh, please don't cry! This doesn't help!

ROSE: (*Struggling*) Now those are my own people outside the door with torches, and I'm not going to move from this house. It's my home. And you can tell them that!

BRIDIE: (*Decisively*) I'll talk to Mona.

38. EXT. NIGHT.

The scene as before.

BRIDIE: Mona, I want a word with you. What are you doing at this house?

MONA: What are you doing at this house! You ought to be ashamed of yourself going in there and your son on the blanket.

BRIDIE: I'm not ashamed. I'm just sorry. I don't seem to be able to help Brendan, or Rose in there, or you. For God's sake, Mona, go home, and take this crowd with you. This is hardly dignified. (*Pause.*) Rose Walsh lost her home before. These people are friends of mine!

MONA: Friends! I'd be very wary of claiming Joe Walsh for a friend. We all have to make sacrifices, you know. My husband was murdered by the Brits and if his mother was in there right now it wouldn't stop me. It's still Joe Walsh's house.

BRIDIE: My God, Mona, you weren't married long!

JOE: Away on home, you vicious wee hussy.

HELEN: Joe, stop it! It won't help calling her names.

BRIDIE: (*Moving closer to* HELEN) I suppose they won't do anything as long as I'm here.

HELEN: I wouldn't be too confident about that, after what she's just said.

BRIDIE: I tried ringing Frank earlier but I couldn't get any answer. I could try again.

(*A car screeches to a halt in the middle of the crowd. They move back.*)

JOE: Who's this now?

HELEN: Oh Christ! Let it not be bad news.

(*Car door slams.* FATHER OLIVER *gets out.*)

FATHER OLIVER: Go to your homes! Go to your homes! It's over. Go to your homes!

BRIDIE: It's Father Oliver. Something's happened at the Kesh. (*To* HELEN) Go and get your mammy.

(HELEN *moves off to the door. All attention is focused on* FATHER OLIVER.)

FATHER OLIVER: Leave these people and go in peace. The Hunger Strike has ended.

MONA: What's that! You have no authority here.

FATHER OLIVER: (*He sees* BRIDIE *for the first time.*) Bridie! I've come from the Maze. It's over. The Hunger Strike is over. Frank's at the prison already. He said you might be here.

BRIDIE: Oh sweet God! Oh sweet God!

(HELEN *and* ROSE *appear behind* BRIDIE.)

FATHER OLIVER: Did you hear me Mona? Now, you go home and take your people with you. It's all over.

MONA: Your jurisdiction stops at the steps of St Michael's. You can't tell me when to go home!

HELEN: (*Moving in towards* MONA) He says it's over Mona. Did you not hear?

MONA: Where's the proof?

FATHER OLIVER: I've come from the prison. (*Takes an A4 two-page statement from his pocket.*) This statement from the Secretary of State has just been read to all men on the Hunger Strike and all other protesting prisoners. It sets out what will happen when they come off the protest. And they've accepted. (*Reaction of amazement from the demonstrators.*) The Hunger Strikers are now being fed.

MONA: Are you telling me that the Brits have given in on Special Category status?

FATHER OLIVER: No. I'm not saying that.

MONA: But then what is happening? What have they accepted?

JOE: Read it out. Read the statement out.

FATHER OLIVER: Listen. I'll read some of it out. Listen to this. 'Within a few days clothing provided by their own families will be given to any prisoners giving up their protest so they can wear it during recreation, association and visits. As soon as possible, all prisoners will be issued with civilian-type clothing for wear during the day . . .'

MONA: This is a trick!

JOE: It's no trick. That's what's written down there and that's what they've accepted.

BRIDIE: I don't understand what's happening. He says it's over, but they wouldn't come off the Hunger Strike without their demands being met.

HELEN: Joe, what's happening?

JOE: It's what they were offered on the fourth of December.

MONA: They were fools to agree to this!

HELEN: But they have, Mona. And it's their lives.

(*The* PRIEST *approaches them.*)

FATHER OLIVER: Come on, now. You take your people home. (*To the crowd*) It's a time to celebrate. It's a miracle of prayer.

MONA: (*Ignores him.*) You're lucky, Joe Walsh! You're lucky that tomorrow we'll be organizing a celebration march and not Sean McKenna's funeral! How can you sleep in your bed at night with your conscience –

JOE: (*Calls.*) Away on home, you wee –

HELEN: Joe! For God's sake!

ROSE: Joe!

FATHER OLIVER: (*Standing in the road talking to the crowd*) It's a victory for you. Go to your homes. They're going to live. Your sons and your daughters are going to live. You've got what you wanted. Go home now.

MONA: We go home – but because we choose to go home and not because you send us.

ROSE: It's over then Joe. Is it?

JOE: Aye, it's all over.

(*The crowd withdraws.* BRIDIE *is standing by* HELEN *watching them.* JOE *has his arm around* ROSE *standing at the front door. The* PRIEST *is in the middle of the street facing the crowd also.*)

BRIDIE: (*To* HELEN, *but also to herself*) It's a victory. They're going to live.

(*The* PRIEST *turns and comes towards her. His car is still parked by the pavement.*)

FATHER OLIVER: Come on now, Bridie. Brendan's been asking for you. I'll take you to the prison.

39. EXT. GATE. NIGHT.

HELEN *at the gate, watching the crowd withdrawing. She is alone.*

HELEN: Sometimes I get so tired of the weight of being Irish.

40. INT. WALSHES' LIVING ROOM. NIGHT.

Walshes' living room. JOE *has settled by the fire.* ROSE *comes in from the backyard with a shovel of coal. He looks up.*

JOE: Did I tell you, Rose? Your bins will be emptied tomorrow.
ROSE: (*Puts the coal on.*) Och you don't say? When did you hear?
JOE: It was settled this afternoon. There's to be no more redundancies, so they're back to working normal time. I told them I wasn't going home without a settlement, my wife would give me no peace.
ROSE: (*Smiles at him.*) Och sure that's great. I hate a dirty yard at Christmas.

41. EXT. GATE. NIGHT.

HELEN *at the gate alone watching the lights of the crowd withdrawing.*

HELEN: (*Voice over*) I still remember that time on the road to Derry when I ran a gauntlet of rocks and stones and one of them struck me. I still have the scar somewhere. I still get headaches. (*Pause.*) Colm was ten when the troubles started. He stood there looking at his uncle lying in the road. He didn't know what it was about, but he knew he was in.

42. INT. WALSHES' LIVING ROOM. NIGHT.

Walshes' living room. JOE *is peering out of the window again.* ROSE, *turning to look at* JOE.

ROSE: What's she doing out there, Joe?
(*He does not turn, nor does he answer.*)

43. EXT. GATE. NIGHT.

HELEN *at the gate, looking up the street. The last flicker of torches leaves the top of the road.*

HELEN: (*Voice over*) I still remember that time when we thought we were beginning a new journey: the long march. What we didn't see was that it had begun a long time before with someone else's journey; we were simply getting through the steps in our own time. (JOE*'s face at the window.*) What we didn't see was that we never had a time which we could call our own.

44. INT. WALSHES' LIVING ROOM. NIGHT.

Walshes' living room. JOE *has turned to* ROSE.

JOE: She appears to be looking at the moon.

45. EXT. NIGHT.

The moon over West Belfast.

A WOMAN CALLING

CHARACTERS

LAURA	Aged 30, 18 and 11
PROFESSOR BRODERICK	
BRODERICK'S COLLEAGUE	
JOHN BURKE	
SHEELAGH BURKE	Aged 12
PEGGY	
MORAIG	
MRS BURKE	
MR BURKE	
LAURA'S FATHER	
LAURA'S MOTHER	
MR GRAHAM	Plain clothes policeman
MR NICHOLL	Plain clothes policeman
FIRST MAN	
SECOND MAN	
THIRD MAN	
JOHN MULHERNE	Laura's boyfriend at 18
LINDA	Friend of Laura's at 18
MARION	Friend of Laura's at 18
DOCTOR	

The play is set in County Down in a house at the coast. The time is December 1982 and there are flashbacks to 1961 and Belfast in 1968.

A Woman Calling was first shown on BBC 2 Television on 18 April 1984 and the cast was as follows:

LAURA (30 and 18)	Paula Hamilton
PROFESSOR BRODERICK	Tony Doyle
BRODERICK'S COLLEAGUE	Denys Hawthorne
LAURA (11)	Tracey Lynch
JOHN BURKE	Robin Cameron
SHEELAGH BURKE	Cathy Brennan
PEGGY	Sheila McGibbon
MORAIG	Deirdre Morgan
MRS BURKE	Kate McClay
MR BURKE	Ian McElhinney
LAURA'S FATHER	Louis Rolston
LAURA'S MOTHER	Leila Webster
MR GRAHAM	Derek Lord
MR NICHOLL	Derek Halligan
FIRST MAN	John Hewitt
SECOND MAN	Michael Duffy
THIRD MAN	Birdie Sweeney
JOHN MULHERNE	Ewan Stewart
LINDA	Aingeal Grehan
MARION	Mary Jackson
DOCTOR	John Keyes
Producer	Chris Parr
Director	Sarah Pia Anderson
Camera	Sam Wilson
Lighting	John Mason
Designer	John Armstrong

I. INT. AN EMPTY ROOM. DAY.

An empty room, overlooking the sea. Early evening. The door opens but we do not see who has entered the room. The camera angle sweeps the room. It is a study with many books lining the walls. The unseen occupant of the room moves to the window. The view from the window is of the sea.

FEMALE: (*Voice over*) I have a strange story to tell. Even now it is not easy for me to remember how much I actually did hear or see, and how much I imagined. The journey between the shore of memory and the landfall of imagination is an unknown distance, because for each voyager it is a passage through a different domain. This story has a little to do with mapping that passage, but only a little: it is also a confession.
(*The view gradually darkens with the speaking voice until there is only night.*)

2. INT. QUEEN'S UNIVERSITY. BELFAST 1982. NIGHT.

Two middle-aged men enter a lecture theatre full of students. One is PROFESSOR BRODERICK, *the other is a* COLLEAGUE.

COLLEAGUE: I'd like you to welcome this evening Professor Broderick, who is visiting the Faculty from New York.
(*Applause as* PROFESSOR BRODERICK *takes his place at the podium.* BRODERICK*'s lecture on memory in dreams is in two parts: a leisurely introduction reinforcing key themes in the first part: and a summing up of his own position in the second half.*)
BRODERICK: According to Freud, dreaming is another form of remembering though one that is subject to the conditions that rule at night. I want to look here at the tyranny of dreams, their power, in particular the power of dreams to cast a spell over a life. Nothing that is memorized is ever

forgotten; even the most insignificant event leaves an unalterable trace: we do not dream trivially. So we are told over and over. Yet I come here to bury Freud, not to praise him.
(*Pause. Laughter from the students.*)
It has been a long established principle of Freud's work that the story is the cure – what we have called the talking of the story. At the very core is the principle of catharsis, through the re-enacting of the memory of the trauma, the sufferer – the hysterical woman, the precocious child – will find a release. The nature of analysis has been to uncover a memory whose secret is held in dreams. But whose dreams do we dream? Where do they come from?

3. EXT. A LARGE HOUSE. NIGHT.

A large house on or near the shore line of County Down between Belfast and Bangor.
PROFESSOR BRODERICK *drives up to the front of the house. The car tyres crunch slowly over the gravel drive which runs along the front of the house as the car stops.*

4. INT. HOUSE. NIGHT.

Continuous time. PROFESSOR BRODERICK *goes into the hall. It is a long hall with a flight of stairs ahead. The hall table, above which stands a mirror, has several newspapers on it. The date on the paper is December 1982, and the leading headline refers to the GLC invitation to Sinn Fein. On the front page of the same newspaper is a photograph of* BRODERICK, *with the caption: 'Professor Broderick returns home on Lecture Tour'. He regards his face in the mirror, comparing it with the photograph. He picks up a copy of a book from the table:* History and Imagination *by John Broderick. He then goes upstairs carrying the book.* PROFESSOR BRODERICK *turns at* [illegible] *first landing. He walks along the passage to a room with a light* [illegible] *opens the door.*

5. INT. ROOM. NIGHT.

Continuous time. PROFESSOR BRODERICK *walks to his desk to put the book down. He is wearing a belted trenchcoat which he has not yet removed. He looks up and sees a girl, the unseen occupant of the room: she is standing by the window with her back to him. He is startled.*

LAURA, *although 33, has a very young appearance. She is very vividly dressed in fantasy colours. She has not turned her head to him yet. He stands regarding her. The overall effect is of a young and pretty female. Her shoes catch his attention, flat with a tiny strap like those of a young girl. Laura's colours are brighter than the plum Victorian interior of Broderick's study. All this* BRODERICK *the psychologist takes in at a glance.*

BRODERICK: I –

(*She turns to look at him. Her face is the face of a woman. He realizes his mistake at once in thinking her so young.*)

Where did you come from?

LAURA: The door was open.

BRODERICK: Who are you?

LAURA: Don't you recognize me, Professor? I recognize you. Your picture's in all the papers.

(*Very jerky unsure movement of her hands.* BRODERICK *notices the bandage.*)

BRODERICK: You were at the lecture. Were you?

LAURA: Fame must be awful strange – all those letters from cranks asking for money. People coming up to you in the street and saying – I remember you at school, you were an awful wee shit. If I were famous, I'm sure they'd say that about me. At school anyway. All those misrememberings!

BRODERICK: What is it you want?

LAURA: I think you can cure me.

BRODERICK: Of what?

LAURA: Of a dream.

BRODERICK: I'm sorry, they should have told you I'm not that kind of analyst.

LAURA: Please. I only want to talk. Only you can help.

BRODERICK: What happened to your hand?

LAURA: I bit it.

BRODERICK: You bit it?

LAURA: Yes. Last night in a dream I saw my enemy's hand before my face – so I bit it, hard. And when I woke up I had this cut.

BRODERICK: (*Interested*) What is your name?

LAURA: Laura.

BRODERICK: Sit down.

(*She looks around.*)

Why don't you sit here.

(*He indicates a* chaise longue *near him.*)

LAURA: I know this place. I came to a house not far from here over twenty years ago across the lough – when I was thirteen.

(*She says this moving across the room to the sofa.*)

BRODERICK: Why don't you relax.

LAURA: Relax.

(*She smiles and sits down.*)

It was at the end of my first year at the convent and Sheelagh Burke invited me to spend the summer at her family home.

BRODERICK: Take your time –

(*He begins to take off his coat.*)

6. INT. HOUSE. DAY.

Summer. LAURA *is standing before a large house similar to the one* BRODERICK *has just entered. By day the similarity need not be so evident. Suddenly as she reaches for the bell and rings it, the door is swung open. She stands face to face with a* YOUNG MAN *whose face breaks into a smile. He is looking down at her. She does not have time to respond before he darts off down the steps to the side of the house and disappears.*

7. INT. HOUSE. DAY.

Continuous time. LAURA *goes into the hall with two bags. She stands alone in the hallway, and seems dwarfed by the size. Suddenly footsteps are heard running heavily downstairs. A door on the right opens noisily,* PEGGY *appears from the cloakroom.*

SHEELAGH: Laura! You're here.
(LAURA *begins to shake hands with* PEGGY.)
PEGGY: Did you have a nice journey down?
LAURA: Yes thank you, Mrs Burke. It was very kind of you to ask me. My mammy said I'm to be no trouble to you, and if you'd like me to stay on longer than the five weeks, I can. She doesn't need me in the shop, they've got extra help. She asked me to give you this.
(PEGGY *and* SHEELAGH *are staring at her.* SHEELAGH *begins to snigger.* PEGGY *takes the parcel.*)
PEGGY: Thank you, Laura.
SHEELAGH: She's not my mother. This is Peggy, our housekeeper.
LAURA: Oh. Well, you can have the chocolates anyway. I'll buy some more for Mrs Burke. I've got plenty of money.
(SHEELAGH *sniggers again.*)
SHEELAGH: Come on, I'll show you your bedroom.
(*They take a bag each and climb the stairs.*)
You're still wearing ankle socks!
LAURA: I know – but, you know what my mother's like.
SHEELAGH: Never mind. I have lots of tights. You can have a pair of mine.
(*A girl in her twenties passes them on the stairs carrying laundry. She nods.*)
LAURA: Who was that?
SHEELAGH: Moraig.
(LAURA *is overwhelmed by the size of the house as they climb the stairs.*)
LAURA: Does she live here too?
SHEELAGH: Yes, in the basement, Peggy is on the same floor as

us. Worse luck! (*Turns and stops.*) I wear lipstick now.

LAURA: Yes, I noticed.

(*At the top of the stairs they pass the open door of a bedroom, a room similarly placed to Broderick's study.* LAURA *has a clear view of the sea.*)

Look at that!

SHEELAGH: That's my brother's room. There's a better view from higher up.

8. INT. BEDROOM. DAY.

Continuous time. LAURA *and* SHEELAGH *enter a bedroom and put down the bags. The room is a bold rose colour with prints on the walls and matching curtains and covers on the twin beds in the room. The dressing table, which is skirted in white lace, immediately attracts* LAURA*'s attention. She goes to the mirror first. There are three sections. She catches sight of her face, moves the angles of the mirrors and smiles.* SHEELAGH *has gone to the window.*

SHEELAGH: Look. I told you. I told you it was a better view.

(LAURA *moves from the mirror to the window. She drops her gaze to the lawn beneath. She sees two people on the lawn.* MORAIG *is crossing the lawn from the tennis court. The* YOUNG MAN *who passed* LAURA *at the front door earlier approaches her. They meet and talk.*)

You can see our tennis court from here. My father had it built last year. He bought up the next door garden to put it in.

LAURA: Who is that?

SHEELAGH: Where? (*Looks down.*) That's my brother. He's awful. Don't even speak to him. Anyway he's too old for you.

LAURA: I'd better unpack.

SHEELAGH: Oh leave it – Peggy will do that for you.

LAURA: How do we get to the sea from here?

SHEELAGH: We have to climb down by the rocks. You can go through the garden. And we can swim there and nobody can see us.

LAURA: Could we go now? That would be great. Did I tell you I can dive now?

SHEELAGH: I don't believe you.

LAURA: I can!

9. EXT. SEASHORE. DAY.

LAURA *and* SHEELAGH *are swimming.*

LAURA: Are you sure no one can see us?

SHEELAGH: I told you the beach is private, this bit belongs to us!

LAURA: But your brother might come out.

SHEELAGH: Well, he'd hardly be interested in you. Anyway he's going to be a doctor. They see everything. They have to take an oath of secrecy about the things that they see.

LAURA: Do they?

SHEELAGH: Of course.

LAURA: But won't your mammy or daddy mind?

SHEELAGH: They're never here to mind. Anyway I'm allowed. My daddy does it.

LAURA: Oh.

10. EXT. SEASHORE. DAY.

Continuous time. The girls are swimming when PEGGY *appears through the garden door on to the rocks. She begins waving and shouting at them.*

PEGGY: Come out of that water this minute.
(*She picks up the bathing towels.*)

SHEELAGH: Pretend you haven't heard her.
(PEGGY *is waving and shouting.*)

PEGGY: Come out of that now. Come out of that water this minute. Do you hear me! You come out this minute! Wait till your father hears about this.

(*In the water a little off shore.*)

LAURA: Oh, I really think we ought to go, she's very cross.

PEGGY: Sheelagh Burke! I'll tell your father. Come out immediately.

SHEELAGH: Oh all right. Why did you have to turn round and see her.

(*They swim towards her and climb out of the water on to the rocks.* PEGGY *is standing holding a towel, she puts it around* SHEELAGH *who is first out.*)

PEGGY: So this is how you're going to carry on with your friend here. (*Wrapping the other towel around* LAURA) Swimming without anything on. I never heard the like. I'll send her right back to Belfast in the morning.

LAURA: She told me it was all right.

SHEELAGH: My father does it. He says it's all right.

PEGGY: Your father said nothing of the sort, Madam.

SHEELAGH: He did. He said what's the good of having your own beach if you can't swim in your birthday suit.

11. EXT. GARDEN OF HOUSE. DAY.

PEGGY *chases* SHEELAGH *and* LAURA *up the garden towards the house.*

PEGGY: Get away on of that with you. I never heard the like of it. Never in all my born days.

(MORAIG *is closing the window on the first floor. This is the same position that* LAURA *had taken up in Broderick's study at the beginning of the play.* LAURA *watches her for a second before hurrying on. Hold on* MORAIG'*s face at the window.*)

12. INT. THE ROOM. NIGHT.

Return to the interview in the room, between LAURA *and* BRODERICK.

LAURA: I was so happy then. I'd never been in a house like that before. I'd never seen rooms like that anywhere. It was as if some great life had to be lived there in those rooms – and yet, it was so empty. Peggy was the only one who took any notice of us. Sheelagh's brother was around at weekends – and there was Moraig.

(*Rapid movement of her hands during this statement.*)

BRODERICK: What age was Moraig?

LAURA: (*Puzzled*) What age? Fifteen or sixteen. I think. I've never been very good at that. Telling people's ages. She'd just left school. So she must have been. But we didn't see much of her. We didn't see much of any of them. Sheelagh's father flew in and out of the country so often it made my head spin. Places like Zurich, Munich and New York cropped up in the conversation by way of explaining his disappearances. And you know for a long time I never saw her mother. It was odd to me, because if I lived in a house like that, I thought, I should never want to go away and leave it. And in the beginning it was true. I dreaded going home again – and then everything changed.

13. INT. BEDROOM. NIGHT.

LAURA *is standing at the dressing-table mirror making-up her eyes. She is not aware that* JOHN BURKE *is standing at the bedroom door watching.*

JOHN BURKE: Ah! Ah! Ah!

(*She suddenly sees him in the mirror. She drops the eye-liner she is holding, and knocks over a bottle of make-up in her confusion. He comes into the room towards her.*)

What's all the hurry?

(LAURA *turns to face him.*)

You don't need it.

(LAURA *is speechless with embarrassment. She continues to stare up at him. He turns to go.*)

If Peggy catches you she'll wash your face.

(He goes out leaving LAURA *staring after him. Her expression says nothing. Focus on* LAURA*'s face.)*

14. INT. MUSIC ROOM. NIGHT.

With the same expression she opens the door to the music room: a long rectangular room running from front to back of the house. Full-length windows fill the short walls at either end. There is a wide marble fireplace with a china doll at each end and a mirror above the mantelpiece. The fire is lit. SHEELAGH *is sitting on the sofa. A very elegant woman is standing in front of the mirror at the fireplace looking at herself. In addition to the make-up,* LAURA *is wearing a long dress, a cloak, and carrying a paper bag. She gasps at the sight of the woman.*

MRS BURKE: *(Coming towards her)* Hello. You must be Sheelagh's little friend.

LAURA: Hello.

MRS BURKE: How nice of you to come.

(She turns to look at SHEELAGH *once more, before leaving the room.)*

SHEELAGH: *(Getting up quickly)* What kept you?

LAURA: I had to get myself ready.

*(*SHEELAGH *goes to the sofa and gets down on her hands and knees.)*

Who was that woman?

SHEELAGH: *(Bringing out a flask and a snack box from underneath the sofa.)* My mother.

LAURA: Your mother?

SHEELAGH: She doesn't live here with us. She was just visiting.

LAURA: Oh. I thought we were done for.

SHEELAGH: Sure, she never notices anything. *(She starts opening the snack box, begins also to pour the soup.)* What have you got in the bag?

LAURA: The other bits of my costume.

(She settles down on the floor.)

SHEELAGH: Here. These sausages are cold, but the soup's warm. You could dip your sausages in it.

LAURA: What is it?
SHEELAGH: Tomato.

(LAURA *sips her soup.*)

LAURA: It's nice.
SHEELAGH: What one are you going to tell?
LAURA: Wheels on the gravel.
SHEELAGH: I don't remember that. How does it go?
LAURA: I haven't told this one before.
SHEELAGH: Do you remember that time at school when you told the ghost story about the bells, and Carmela Madden was standing outside the commonroom door with the nuns' bell; every time you mentioned the word bell she rang it!
LAURA: Yeah. And Catherine Divine went into hysterics! (*They both collapse laughing.*)
SHEELAGH: And do you remember she rang it five times and Mother Dominica came rushing down because that's the number of bells they ring in the convent to call her.
LAURA: And we all got caught on, yeah. It was all right for you – you're a fee payer. She said she was going to put me out of school if I ever did anything like that again. (SHEELAGH *is still laughing.*)
SHEELAGH: Och, sure it was great.
LAURA: Well, are we ready?
SHEELAGH: Yeah. I'm listening.

(LAURA *takes another slurp of the soup; it leaves a red residue around her mouth. Then she gets to her feet to act the story out.*)

LAURA: One night many years ago in the countryside of South Tyrone, a family were awaiting the return of their only son who had left home to make his fortune in America many years before . . .

(*Fade out and in during this scene: the clock in the room indicates ten minutes past ten.*)

It was winter and so it was dark, country dark, there was no moon and very few stars about . . .

(*Fade out to the night sky through the window, and back into the room again.*)

Almost immediately on the last chime of the expected hour

the sound of carriage wheels on the gravel drive outside the house was heard.
(*She pauses to take off the storyteller's cloak. She is wearing a long dress underneath.*)
The mother who heard this, turned to her maid and said: 'He has come at last, go and let him in. Now we can go to dinner.'
(*She pauses and puts on an apron which she takes from the bag.*)
The maid left the room, but returned very quickly: 'Madam,' she said. 'There is no one at the door.'
(*She takes the apron off.*)
'But I heard,' the mother protested. 'I heard the carriage wheels very distinctly.'
(*She puts on the apron again.*)
'I am sorry, Madam,' said the maid, who was very nervous, and not used to contradicting the woman of the house. 'But there is no one at the door.'
(*She takes off the apron and puts on a man's top hat.*)
The woman's husband, overhearing all of this, looked very worried, and said to his wife: 'What time is it?'
(*She takes off the hat.*)
'Just turned seven o'clock,' his wife answered.
(*She puts on the hat again.*)
'Then prepare yourself for bad news,' her husband told her. 'Because you have heard too soon, our son will never arrive, not now, not tomorrow, nor any other day! By your impatience, woman, your impatient desire, you have caused our son's death!'
(*She takes off the hat and puts on the cloak.*)
That night the woman went to bed with a great sorrow on her heart, and in the morning a messenger confirmed what her husband has said.

SHEELAGH: Wait a minute, I don't understand this.

LAURA: I haven't finished.

SHEELAGH: I know, but I don't understand it.

LAURA: What bit do you not understand?

SHEELAGH: How is it his mother's fault?

LAURA: She heard his carriage wheels on gravel because she

wanted to hear them at that time. Even though they weren't there. She should have waited and let them come in their own time. It was a bad omen.

SHEELAGH: Oh.

LAURA: At precisely the moment when the carriage wheels turned on the gravel the boy died –

(The sound of a car drawing up on the gravel during this statement causes them both to turn to the front window. LAURA*'s voice trails away.* SHEELAGH *has half eaten a sausage. She stares up at* LAURA *as the noise continues.)*

SHEELAGH: Oh stop it.

(The sound of wheels is more pronounced. They appear to be slowly edging past the window.)

Make it stop! *(Shaking* LAURA.)

LAURA: I'm not doing anything.

(The car stops suddenly. SHEELAGH *jumps up and puts her hands over her ears and runs from the room.)*

SHEELAGH: Oh God. Oh God. Oh God.

(The door slams leaving LAURA *standing in the middle of the room. The vibration of the door closing causes a small china doll to topple from the mantelpiece into the hearth and shatter.* LAURA *gets down on her knees beside the broken figure and fingers the pieces.)*

LAURA: It's broken.

15. INT. LANDING. NIGHT.

PEGGY *comes to the landing, holding the banister rail, and looks downstairs into the dark hall. She listens, unsure.*

PEGGY: Moraig! Is that you?

(She listens again, and then goes downstairs very cautiously.)

16. INT. ROOM. NIGHT.

Continuous time. LAURA *is sitting in terrified silence watching the firelight throw shadows on to the wall opposite. She begins to watch the door handle. She imagines it is turning. She closes her eyes. She is still sitting in front of the fire in the room when she opens her eyes. She begins to yawn. As she does a small gasp is heard from the fire. She puts her hand to her mouth and listens. This time she is not yawning and the sound is very clear.*

VOICE: Hah . . . hah . . . hah . . . hah.
(LAURA *sits up rigid. The sound seems to die away for a moment and then become louder.*)
Hah . . . hah . . . hah. Hah. Hah.
(LAURA *leaps up and runs screaming from the room.*)

17. INT. HALL AND STAIRS. NIGHT.

LAURA *dashes upstairs.*

LAURA: Oh Jesus! Oh Jesus!
(*She runs straight into* PEGGY *half-way upstairs, and ends up clinging to her.*)
PEGGY: What in heaven's name's the matter with you! And what are you doing dressed up like that?
LAURA: Oh Jesus! Oh Jesus!
PEGGY: Will you stop that now and tell me what the matter is!
LAURA: I won't do it again. I won't do it again.
(PEGGY *shakes her.*)
PEGGY: Stop that! Isn't it as well I came down. You should have been in bed hours ago. And where's Miss Sheelagh Burke?
LAURA: I dunno. She ran away and left me in the dark. I want my mammy. I want to go home.
PEGGY: Now listen to me, Madam. You'll go straight back to Belfast tomorrow if there's any more carry on. Screaming and bringing the house down.
(PEGGY *suddenly looks closely at* LAURA.)
And what have you got on your face?
(LAURA *stares blankly back.*)
Here.
(PEGGY *takes out a hanky from her sleeve and puts it to her*

mouth and wets it. She begins to wipe Laura's face.)
I don't know what Mr Burke would say if he knew.
(LAURA *resists at first.*)

LAURA: Sheelagh says her daddy doesn't care what she does.

PEGGY: Oh does she now! You don't want to take any notice of what Sheelagh says. Hold still.
(LAURA *allows* PEGGY *to wipe away some of her eye make-up.*)

LAURA: I wish my daddy didn't care what I did.

PEGGY: That's better.

LAURA: He's awful cross sometimes. He's not like you, you only sound cross.
(PEGGY *is a little taken aback.*)

PEGGY: Oh do I indeed!
(*Taking* LAURA *upstairs*) Come on now. It's time you were in bed.

LAURA: Can I keep the light on? I don't like the dark.
(PEGGY *and* LAURA *disappear into the darkness at the top of the stairs.*)

18. INT. THE ROOM. NIGHT.

Return to the scene in the room between LAURA *and* BRODERICK.

LAURA: Sleep. I am always afraid to go to sleep and have been ever since that time. It has something to do with going to sleep with one reality and waking up with another. It was like this on that particular morning.

19. INT. BEDROOM. DAY.

Laura's bedroom and the morning view of the sea, and of the bedroom when PEGGY *enters carrying a cup of tea.*

LAURA: (*Sitting up in bed*) Where's Sheelagh?

PEGGY: Oh, she was up hours ago.

LAURA: Why didn't she wake me?

PEGGY: Because you were sleeping, that's why. Now be a good girl and hurry up and get dressed. There are two gentlemen downstairs who would like to talk to you.

LAURA: To me? Are you sure?

(PEGGY *is moving around the room picking up clothes.*)

PEGGY: That should have been in the wash.

(LAURA *gets quickly out of bed and goes to the washstand basin.*)

LAURA: Peggy? What do they want to talk to me about?

PEGGY: They just want to ask you a few questions. And Mr Burke has come back today. He's downstairs as well.

(*She pull her nightdress off over her head, turning away from* PEGGY *to do so. She then pulls a sweatshirt on.*)

Do you call that washing yourself? That was a lick and a rub. Isn't it as well I came up. (*Moves to the basin.*) Come here.

LAURA: (*Resisting*) I'll wash afterwards.

PEGGY: (*Shakes her head.*) I don't understand you wee girls at all. You'd think you were afraid of water!

LAURA: Mother Dominica always says gentlemen when she means policemen.

PEGGY: Now what makes you say that?

LAURA: When Carmela Madden's gold watch went missing Mother Dominica called in two gentlemen to ask us questions. It's always the day girls she picks on – never the boarders. They found her watch on the tennis court where she'd taken it off. Why have you called the police? I haven't stolen anything.

PEGGY: Good gracious! What a silly wee thing. Of course you haven't.

LAURA: Then why are there two policemen downstairs wanting to ask me questions?

PEGGY: They only want to see if you can help them.

LAURA: How?

PEGGY: We'll just have to go down and find out.

20. INT. STAIRS. DAY.

At the foot of the stairs outside the family's other reception room.

LAURA: Where's Moraig? She usually brings my tea in the morning.
(PEGGY *opens the door into the room. There are three men in the room:* MR BURKE, *and the two policemen,* MR GRAHAM *and* MR NICHOLL. LAURA *hesitates momentarily before coming into the room. During the introductions she catches sight briefly of the scene outside the front window. There are two uniformed policemen and two civilians moving about outside the window.*)

GRAHAM: Hello, Laura, I am Mr Graham and this is my friend, Mr Nicholl.
(LAURA *shakes hands with both of them.* MR BURKE *remains a little removed from the situation.*)
We want you to tell us what it was that made you scream out last night.
(LAURA, *panic-stricken, turns to* PEGGY.)

LAURA: You called the police because I screamed?
(*She makes an attempt to run from the room, but* PEGGY *holds her back.*)

PEGGY: No love, that's not it at all.

LAURA: I haven't done anything wrong.

PEGGY: Of course you haven't.

BURKE: Laura. You haven't met me before. I'm Sheelagh's father.

LAURA: (*Solemnly*) Hello.

BURKE: I want you to tell Mr Graham what happened last night. No one is going to hurt you.
(PEGGY *squeezes her arm.*)

PEGGY: Go on. There's a good girl.
(LAURA *bursts into tears.*)

LAURA: I didn't mean anything. I want my mammy. I want to go home, please.

PEGGY: Oh come on now. You can go home today. There, there.

GRAHAM: (*To* NICHOLL) This is useless. She's even worse than the other wee girl.

BURKE: Laura! All you have to do is tell us why you ran out of that room screaming last night.

NICHOLL: You were telling stories?

(GRAHAM *indicates to* NICHOLL *to be quiet.*)

LAURA: Yes. I was telling a ghost story and we got frightened because the car drove up.

GRAHAM: What car?

(LAURA *nods her head towards the front window.*)

LAURA: Out there.

GRAHAM: Did you see what type of car it was?

LAURA: No. It wasn't there.

(NICHOLL *and* MR BURKE *begin to look impatient.*)

GRAHAM: But if it wasn't there, how did you hear it?

LAURA: Because it was part of the story.

(GRAHAM *looks baffled.*)

I was telling a ghost story when it happened. We both heard it drive over the gravel and Sheelagh ran away and left me in the dark. I was too scared to go to bed so I stayed there.

NICHOLL: Did you go to the window and look out? Was that what made you scream?

LAURA: No. It was the voices.

NICHOLL: What voices?

LAURA: I heard voices, but there was no one in the room but me – and I wasn't talking.

NICHOLL: What kind of voices? Where?

LAURA: (*She points.*) They came out of the fire.

NICHOLL: You heard voices in the fire?

LAURA: Yes.

(NICHOLL *looks at* GRAHAM.)

I didn't imagine it. I heard it. And I heard the wheels outside as well.

GRAHAM: What exactly did the voices say to you, Laura?

LAURA: Nothing.

GRAHAM: Well, what did you hear?

LAURA: It was like calling. It was like a woman calling.
GRAHAM: What did she say?
LAURA: Nothing. No words, just sounds.
GRAHAM: Can you repeat the sounds you think you heard?
LAURA: I don't know.
GRAHAM: Try.
(LAURA *inhales deeply and makes a sucking sound.*)
LAURA: Hah . . . hah . . . hah . . . hah . . . hah . . . hah –
(*Stops, out of breath.*)
GRAHAM: Why did you stop?
LAURA: I didn't hear any more.

21. INT. THE ROOM. DAY.

Return to the interview in the room, between BRODERICK *and* LAURA. *She has her feet tucked up under her.*

LAURA: Mr Burke made his first and last appearance into my life that day. When the interview was over he drove me to the station and I did go home after all. I would have been glad enough about it except I felt I was going home in some disgrace and I wasn't exactly sure why. Sheelagh spoke very little to me; she seemed very down and she told me that she was being sent to an aunt in the West of Ireland for the rest of the summer.
(*She shivers involuntarily.*)
I'm cold. Do you have a rug?
BRODERICK: Of course.
(*He picks up a rug from an armchair and puts it over her.* LAURA *is lying down on the sofa.*)
LAURA: Thank you. She didn't return to school in September, and she didn't write to me as she promised. The last time I saw her in my life was at a railway station the day I said goodbye. (*Pauses.*) My parents never questioned me about it, coming back so soon. I was sure they would – though they didn't seem particularly pleased to see me.
BRODERICK: But what happened?

LAURA: They never told me, and I didn't ask because somewhere deep down I knew already that something very, very terrible had happened. It was seven years before I found out what. Seven years. It was 1968, I went to Queen's as a first year history student; it was the first year of the disturbances in the city. But I wasn't really interested in politics and I knew very little about what was happening, except that there were mass meetings in the Union, the McMordie Hall and on the streets. As you know, it was the beginning of the Civil Rights Movement. It was the most exciting year of my life; inevitably I fell in love.

22. EXT. ROAD. DAY.

The scene of a police cordon drawn across the road at Linenhall Street, November 1968. LAURA *and* JOHN MULHERNE *are at the front of the demonstrators facing the police cordon. They are saluting an immobile police cordon with cries of* Sieg heil. LAURA*'s voice over the scene above.*

LAURA: John Mulherne was a counterpoint to everything my father with his little shop and his cautious peace-keeping ways stood for. He was so outrageous and angry all the time. He didn't care who he offended. I was at home at my father's shop in North Belfast on the weekend following the first Civil Rights marches Belfast had known.

23. INT. NEWSPAPER SHOP. DAY.

Sunday morning in a newspaper shop below the Cave Hill in North Belfast. It is very windy. Laura's FATHER *is fuming over the early dispatches of the Sunday papers. She is watching him but not speaking. Focus on the newspaper headlines of November 1968.*

FATHER: Fools and troublemakers, that's all they are. We have a fine peaceful little country here. What do they want to go making trouble for?

(*He throws down the paper as* THREE MEN *come into the shop. They begin to look over the headlines.*)

FIRST MAN: Good morning, Matt. Hello, Laura.

(*She smiles and takes money from the* THIRD MAN. *Her* FATHER, *Matt, is serving the* SECOND MAN. *The* FIRST MAN *is smoking a pipe and looking at the headlines of the paper in front of him.*)

It's about time O'Neill got rid of that Minister of Home Affairs, and put his money where his mouth is.

SECOND MAN: Aye. But you know, they say he's afraid of the hardliners in the party.

FATHER: Ah now, Mr O'Neill's a great man. He's the best Prime Minister this country's ever had.

THIRD MAN: He sends his daughters to a convent. Did you know that?

SECOND MAN: He's not the same O'Neill. You're thinking of the brother.

FATHER: He's not the brother, he's the man's uncle.

THIRD MAN: That's just the trouble, the government's full of O'Neills. It's very confusing.

FIRST MAN: But do you not think it's wrong that the Unionists should always be the government?

SECOND MAN: It's a one-party state.

THIRD MAN: Aye. It's a one-party state all right. It's what Hitler wanted – total power.

FIRST MAN: But he didn't last fifty years!

THIRD MAN: And do you know how they've done it?

SECOND MAN: They've gerrymandered Derry!

THIRD MAN: They've discredited the opposition.

FATHER: I'm not interested in politics. I can't afford a political viewpoint.

LAURA: That is a political viewpoint. Pure petit bourgeois self-interest.

(*There is silence in the shop. Everyone has turned to look at her. Her* FATHER *is livid. Sound of the wind on the mountain is heard through the silence of this scene.*)

FIRST MAN: That's the stuff. You young ones with your

education will tell them boys at Stormont where to get off.

FATHER: If that's all the good a university education has done you, I rue the day you ever went to that place.

(*She rushes out to the back of the shop, where her* MOTHER *is.*)

MOTHER: What's wrong?

(*Laura's* FATHER *follows her in, slamming the door.*)

Matt, what's wrong?

FATHER: This one, she's what's wrong. Your mother and I broke our backs scraping and saving to give you a chance. If this is how you repay us you can take yourself off; but don't ever come here again shaming me in front of my friends!

(*They both seem to watch her from a great distance.*)

24. INT. THE ROOM. NIGHT.

Return to the scene in the room between LAURA *and* BRODERICK.

LAURA: I moved out of the house after that and went to live permanently on the Lisburn Road with some other students. And then on the sixth of January we came back to Belfast after the march had taken four days to reach Derry. We were attacked at Burntollet Bridge.

BRODERICK: Yes, I know. I was in the States at the time. I read of it.

LAURA: I had not slept with John before that night.

25. INT. BEDROOM. NIGHT.

Scene in the bedroom in the half-light. The room is lit by a street lamp outside the window. January 1969.

LAURA: Leave the curtain open. I like the light.

(JOHN *gets into bed with her, he seems preoccupied. He kisses her.*)

JOHN: Things will never be the same here.

LAURA: (*Whispers.*) Yes, I know.

(*He begins to kiss her.*)

Sometimes I feel so lonely.

(*He moves over on top of her.*)

(*She sighs.*) Oh John.

(*He kisses her again. We have a view of the back of his head and of her face. She closes her eyes. He kisses her breasts.* LAURA *opens her eyes again and her mouth. He grips her shoulders, raises himself. Again, the view is of the back of him and again focuses on her face.*)

(*Gasps.*) Hah . . . hah . . .

(*She closes her eyes. In response to his movement she continues to gasp.*)

Hah . . . hah . . . hah.

(*He puts his hands on her throat.*)

Hah . . . hah . . .

(*She raises her hands to catch his arms.*)

Hah . . . hah . . .

JOHN: Yes. Yes.

LAURA: Hah . . .

(*She suddenly opens her eyes and begins to scream out in great pain. She continues to scream and struggle until he collapses on top of her.*)

JOHN: (*Whispers.*) Laura! Laura!

LAURA: (*Fights him off.*) No no no.

(*Screaming even more loudly in response to his voice. He gets quickly out of bed to move to the light switch. He turns it on. He is terrified. He remains watching her from the door. She stops screaming when the light comes on, but is breathing deeply from shock.*)

I thought you were someone. Don't go away. Don't go away.

26. INT. HALLWAY. NIGHT.

Two students, LINDA *and* MARION, *are hammering at the bedroom door.*

LINDA: John! Laura. What is it?
MARION: He's murdering her.
LINDA: Laura! John! Open this door!

27. INT. BEDROOM. NIGHT.

JOHN *is still standing by the door, frozen in his stare.*

LAURA: I know it all now. She was murdered. I heard it. He strangled her! He strangled Moraig!
(JOHN *turns to open the door.* MARION *and* LINDA *rush in.* JOHN *is standing naked by the door, he is speechless.* LAURA *begins to weep.*)
LINDA: What the hell are you doing to her?
(*She rushes to* LAURA*'s side.*)
LAURA: Oh, don't you understand. Moraig was murdered. He strangled her.
MARION: She's having hysterics. I'd better call a doctor.
(*She rushes out.*)
LINDA: There, there.
LAURA: I was dreaming with my eyes open. I saw his face.
LINDA: (*To* JOHN) You look awful. What happened?
JOHN: I don't know.
LINDA: What were you doing?
JOHN: We were screwing. She thought I was going to kill her.
LINDA: So did I.
LAURA: That night, he strangled her. And I heard it.
LINDA: (*To* JOHN) You look as though you could do with a drink.

28. INT. BEDROOM. NIGHT.

In the bedroom. JOHN *is now sitting in the chair in a dressing-gown. He has a glass of whiskey in his hand.* LAURA *is lying back in the bed.*

LAURA: John. Are you still there?
JOHN: Yes. I'm still here.
LAURA: Do you forgive me?
JOHN: Yeah. Sure.
(*He puts his head in his hands.*)

29. INT. HALLWAY. NIGHT.

In the hallway of the house at the foot of the stairs, LINDA, MARION *and the* DOCTOR *are standing.*

DOCTOR: I need to contact her parents.
LINDA: It'll be an awful shock to them. They haven't seen her for a long time.
DOCTOR: Hmm. I suppose she was on that march.
MARION: Yes. We all were.
DOCTOR: You know the trouble with you people is you start things you can't finish. You kick open doors and you don't know what's behind them.
LINDA: Thanks. All we wanted was your medicine.
DOCTOR: Well, you got it. The best I can do for her at the moment is to get her to sleep. Make sure she gets another one of these when she wakes up. I'll contact her parents tomorrow and get them to take her home.
(JOHN *comes down the stairs.*)
JOHN: She's asleep.
DOCTOR: You don't look too good yourself. Can I give you anything?
JOHN: No. I'm just a bit shaken. I don't understand it.
DOCTOR: You wouldn't. You people are so casual.
(*He goes.*)
LINDA: He's the wonder of Western Medicine, he is. He's got one answer for everything: the pill. Any pill.
MARION: Aye. As long as we sleep through it. Everything will be all right.
(LINDA, MARION *and* JOHN *are left standing at the bottom of the stairs staring at the closed door.*)

30. INT. THE ROOM. DAY.

LAURA *and* BRODERICK *in the room again.*

LAURA: With the morning my parents came –
(*She begins again to tremble. He puts his hand on hers to stop her.*)
Don't. I'm not cold. I just shiver sometimes.
(*He withdraws his hand.*)
The last communication I'd had with them before that was a letter from my mother. It came a few days after Christmas.

31. INT. FRONT ROOM. DAY.

LAURA *is marking a piece of blue cloth material on which she has already placed a white star. She is holding a compass and protractor.* JOHN *is in the background painting with red paint on to a white placard. The words are:* 'End the Special Powers Act'. *He comes up to her with the paint brush and smears the back of her hand. New Year's Eve, 1968.*

LAURA: Stop that.
(*She wipes the paint away with her hand.*)
JOHN: What are you doing?
LAURA: Marking the angle of the plough.
JOHN: Well, it doesn't have to be that precise. It's only a flag.
LAURA: Yes, it does.
(JOHN *shakes his head and moves away to paint another card. He paints:* 'One Man One – ' *before* LINDA *comes into the room.*)
LINDA: Laura! Letter for you.
LAURA: Thanks.
LINDA: John, this has just come back from the printer. Can you check it through?
(LAURA *looks at the postmark and the handwriting on the front of the envelope and moves away to the window at the far end of the room to read it.*)

You're only to proof-read it. It's too late to change anything.

(LAURA *reacts in pain.*)

LAURA: Ah no.

(LINDA *and* JOHN *both turn.*)

LINDA: It's from her family. They didn't even write to her at Christmas.

JOHN: Oh bloody hell. (*Going towards her*) Laura, what is it? Don't let them upset you like this!

LAURA: Sheelagh Burke is dead.

JOHN: Who?

LAURA: Sheelagh Burke. She was a friend of mine – at school.

(*He looks puzzled.*)

She killed herself. She drove her car over the cliff at Westpoint.

JOHN: I'm sorry. You never mentioned her before.

LAURA: I knew her a long time ago.

JOHN: Well, look, at least they've written to you.

LAURA: Yes.

JOHN: Come on, let's finish the plough.

LAURA: In a minute.

(*He moves away. She looks down at her hands again. They are smeared with red paint. So is the letter.*)

32. INT. THE ROOM. NIGHT.

Return to the interview in the room between LAURA *and* BRODERICK.

LAURA: I seem to remember that the tone of my mother's letter was half reproachful as though in Sheelagh's death was some responsibility of mine. I have two deaths on my hands: Moraig's and Sheelagh's.

BRODERICK: But wait a minute. You said Moraig was murdered; you didn't kill her.

LAURA: I dreamed up her death, just as surely as if I had murdered her.

BRODERICK: But you didn't dream it; you say it happened.

LAURA: It happened – but I haven't told you the rest. One detail is missing.

BRODERICK: Please go on.

LAURA: (*Becoming highly excited*) Don't you see when I was telling Sheelagh about the significance of the wheels on the gravel as a sign of death, the car carrying the murderer drew up. I created the event. What is more, I later heard a woman making love up to the point of strangulation, when I began screaming for her. I heard her cries coming up through the chimney passage because her bed was right next to the boxed-in fireplace in the basement. When I sat with my back to the fire I heard her. But I didn't understand what I'd heard. Seven years later when I was making love for the first time I knew everything.

BRODERICK: Everything?

LAURA: Yes. I opened my eyes one split second before I screamed. I saw something. The face I saw was not the face of my lover.

(*Close up on* BRODERICK*'s face*)

BRODERICK: Whose face did you see?

33. INT. NIGHT.

Flashback: return to the final second of the bed scene. This time showing Laura's lover's face. The face of JOHN MULHERNE *above her suddenly becomes the face of the young* JOHN BURKE. *She visually hallucinates between the two faces. Cut on her scream.*

34. INT. THE ROOM. NIGHT.

Return to the scene in the room between LAURA *and* BRODERICK. *She is watching his face. The visual likeness between the younger* BURKE *and the older* BRODERICK *must now be made clear.*

BRODERICK: (*Sighs.*) Why did you come here with this memory. I find it very painful.

LAURA: Why did I come? You ask me that? I spent three years of my life in a hospital. Did you know?

(*He shakes his head.*)

I can't sleep with the light out; I can't lie in the dark in case I see your face. For three years I took their drugs and their treatments but I kept my secret because I knew that the one thing which would cure me was that one day I would meet you again and confront you with the truth about yourself.

BRODERICK: What truth?

LAURA: You murdered Moraig. You were her lover.

BRODERICK: Your hallucination of one face on to another is not proof of anything.

LAURA: Not proof – truth, Professor Broderick! The truth you know best of all.

BRODERICK: Have you talked to anyone else about this?

LAURA: No. They would think I was mad. But I'm not. And you know it. You only have to confess! Confess – and I'm free.

BRODERICK: Let me give you a better explanation of what happened – one you can live with. A servant girl Moraig was murdered by her lover; and perhaps you heard her cries as you said coming up through the chimney passage.

LAURA: Perhaps! I did!

BRODERICK: Now there is one factor you haven't mentioned. You had a massive crush on your friend's brother. You also knew he was friendly with Moraig, because you sometimes watched him; perhaps you saw them exchanging glances. Isn't it possible that you saw my face when your lover – also called John – was making love to you for the first time because mine was the face you wanted to see?

LAURA: No.

BRODERICK: Yes. You fused the murder of Moraig with the desire to see him.

LAURA: No. No. I saw your face because you murdered her. Why else? You were her secret lover. I know.

BRODERICK: Don't persist with this. You've been ill and you're better now. I've offered you a way out – take it. Most of us dream the same dreams, Laura. And the same nightmares – that's the only consolation we've got. Take it!

LAURA: I can't. I cannot break out of this – (*Struggles for the word*) – nightmare.

(*She begins to weep; he watches her.*)

Oh I am not mad!

(*He approaches her, pulls the blanket away and gets down beside her.*)

BRODERICK: John Mulherne, your lover? What happened to him?

(*He puts his hand on her face, touches her cheek. She stares unblinkingly at him.*)

He didn't wait for you to heal?

LAURA: No. He didn't wait.

(*She is still watching him. He puts his hand on her neck. She closes her eyes. Close-up on* LAURA'S *face.*)

35. INT. QUEEN'S UNIVERSITY BELFAST. NIGHT.

The second and final part of Broderick's lecture.

BRODERICK: I can no more accept that we buried the psyche of the Victorian age in 1901 when we buried Queen Victoria, than I could accept the possibility of a cure through the recovery of a memory; for who knows what fatal smoke we inhale unwittingly from a distant fire. Therefore I have not found it helpful to take the path of Freud and his followers to the source of the primeval fire; most likely when we arrive there we would find that it had cooled imperceptibly a long time before; and the contagion we are suffering has already left its mark; the pain we feel is real pain, we know it – it constricts our breathing. My contention is that we are infected and we remain infected. How we live with that knowledge is a matter of degree. And the only possible role for the sufferer is the mapping out, accounting for; the deliberate and detached setting down of the progress of the experience. It would be a mistake to delude ourselves as Freud has led us to believe – that our liberation is in the balance: our crisis is past, but we still go on dreaming it. What I do remember is that, at the beginning of the sixties, among the small change in my pocket, I could still find the head of the old Queen.

36. INT. THE ROOM. DAY.

The room: LAURA *is standing by the window. She turns her head to survey the empty room.* LAURA*'s voice over.*

LAURA: I looked away from the window and found myself alone in the room.

37. INT. NIGHT.

The lecture has ended. BRODERICK *is standing with his back to the blackboard. He is wearing his belted trenchcoat. His* COLLEAGUE *is with him.*

COLLEAGUE: There's someone here you ought to meet. She has a very interesting case history. She was a student of mine.

BRODERICK: I don't take cases any more. Don't you understand?

COLLEAGUE: But this woman needs to see you. She needs to talk to you.

BRODERICK: (*Sighs.*) Tell her to write –

(*Hold on his face as he begins to smile, very slowly.*)

Fade out